Here Are Additional Clues to Hel[illegible] the Mystery of THE REVENGE OF THE ROBINS FAMILY and Win $10,001.

Chapter 1:

First to arrive...

Chapter 2:

The importance of making a good impression...

Chapter 3:

Appearances can be deceiving...

Chapter 4:

Less than meets the eye...

Chapter 5:

Lookalikes...

Chapter 6:

Prologue to murder...

Chapter 7:

Last to arrive...

The Revenge of the Robins Family

The Revenge of the Robins Family

Created by Bill Adler
Written by Thomas Chastain

Who Killed the Seven Victims and
WHEN and WHERE and HOW and WHY
Did They Die?

Solve the crimes. Win $10,001!

William Morrow and Company, Inc. | New York

Library of Congress Catalog Card Number: 84-60791

ISBN: 0-688-03793-3

Printed in the United States of America

4 5 6 7 8 9 10

OFFICIAL CONTEST RULES

Someone will definitely win $10,001 in *The Revenge of the Robins Family* contest. Will it be you?

Here are the rules: To enter, use ordinary paper. Make sure your name and address are clearly printed at the top of each page of your entry. Print or type your answers to the following six questions for each of the seven unsolved murders:

1. Who was the murder victim?
2. Who was the killer?
3. Where did the murder take place?
4. When did the murder happen?
5. How was the victim killed?
6. Why was the victim killed?

Answer all questions one at a time in the order given above for each of the murders. Each set of six answers must be clearly identified as relating to a single victim. Only entries with complete answers to all six questions for each of the victims are eligible for the reward. Mail your entry, plus 50 cents processing fee (cash, check, or money order), to: Ventura Associates, Inc., P.O. Box 570, Lowell, Indiana 46356. Enter as often as you wish, but each entry must be mailed in a separate envelope, and must be accompanied by the 50 cents processing fee. All entries must be received by June 15, 1985.

This contest is void where prohibited or restricted by law. All federal, state, and local laws and regulations apply. For the name of the contest winner, send a stamped, self-addressed envelope to: The Revenge of the Robins Family Winner, P.O. Box 657, Lowell, Indiana 46356. Requests will not be fulfilled before August 15, 1985 or later than August 15, 1986.

To receive a copy of the authors' solution to the mystery, send a stamped, self-addressed envelope and 25 cents for handling to: The Revenge of the Robins Family Solution, P.O. Box 717, Lowell, Indiana 46356. Requests for solutions will not be fulfilled before August 15, 1985 or later than August 15, 1986.

The $10,001 will be awarded for what is, in the sole determination of the judges, the best solution. Therefore, even if you're not 100 percent sure you're right, you still might come closest and win the $10,001!

Entries will be reviewed by Ventura Associates, Inc., an independent judging organization whose decisions will be final. The correct answers, as determined by the authors, are being held in a sealed vault pending the final date of the contest. If more than one (or no) completely correct solution is received, the final winning entry will be determined by the best answer to the question "Why was the victim killed?" for each of the seven victims. Best answers will be determined first by correctness. Answers will then be evaluated by the authors for logic, clarity of expression, creativity, and neatness.

The winner of the $10,001 will be notified by mail and the reward presented on or before August 15, 1985. No substitutions for the prize will be allowed. Any and all applicable taxes are the responsibility of the winner. The winner may be asked to sign a statement of eligibility and the winner's name and likeness may be used for publicity purposes. Entries are the property of William Morrow and Company, Inc. The contest is open to residents of the United States eighteen years of age or older. Employees and their families of William Morrow and Company, Inc., Warner Books, Bill Adler Books, Inc., the Hearst Corporation, Nelson Doubleday, Inc., Doubleday & Co., Inc., their respective affiliates and advertising agencies, Ventura Associates, Inc., and the authors are not eligible.

AUTHORS' NOTE

THE FOLLOWING PAGES CONTAIN FICTIONAL ACCOUNTS of eight murders. One of these murders is solved before the conclusion of the book. The reader can see from this solved murder how the real clues are separated out from other information revealed—including so-called red herrings—and lead logically to the correct answer of who committed the murder and where and when and how and why this particular victim died.

The other seven murders in the book remain unsolved, a challenge to the reader to examine each and every piece of evidence, test that evidence for its trustworthiness, logically link it to other clues—and so arrive at a logical solution.

In other words, throughout the book there are real

clues, however small, however large, that provide the correct answer—or, if more than one clue is needed, the correct answers—to the seven unsolved murders, and where and when and how and why the victims died.

One final note: *Not every single piece of information* needed to solve the mysteries of the seven murders is contained in these pages. But the clues that will lead the reader to such information are all there.

—Bill Adler
Thomas Chastain

New York City

CAST OF CHARACTERS
(IN ORDER OF APPEARANCE)

JULIAN SHIELDS—President and chairman of the board of the multimillion-dollar Robins Cosmetics; was once the Robins family lawyer.

JANICE SHIELDS—Wife of Julian; British-born, she now lives with her husband at the Greenlawn estate in Maryland.

ALFRED WALES—The Shields butler.

DORINA WALES—The Shields cook-housekeeper, wife of Alfred.

GEORGE PITTMAN—Was married to Libby Robins before her death, currently a member of the Board of Directors of Robins Cosmetics.

PAMELA ROBINS MACGUFFIN—Was married to Marshall Robins; mother of his daughter, Marsha. Currently married to David MacGuffin.

GENEVIEVE ROBINS, ETC.—Was married to James Robins; mother of his daughter, Bettina. Currently remarried. A French beauty and former model.

PAUL BRYCE—Head of Tiempo Cosmetics, a rival of Robins Cosmetics.

ERNEST TRUAX—Former employee of Robins Cosmetics, now working for Paul Bryce.

B. J. GRIEG—A private investigator sometimes employed by Robins Cosmetics.

TAYLOR ROBINS—Twin brother of the dead Tyler Robins.

BENJAMIN ROBINS—Son of Taylor, twin brother of Belden.

BELDEN ROBINS—Identical twin brother of Benjamin, except that Belden has a small V-shaped scar across the bridge of his nose.

CAPTAIN GREGORY WALTHAM—Works in the Homicide Bureau of the Maryland State Police.

MARC ROLLANDE—Second husband of Genevieve; a Frenchman, owner of a Manhattan art gallery.

CARRIE WALES—Daughter of Alfred and Dorina; had a child, Molly, by James Robins.

PIERRE DUPIN—Shady French financier; friend of Marc Rollande.

DAVID MacGUFFIN—Mystery novelist; second husband of Pamela.

REBECCA ROBINS—Wife of Taylor Robins.

JONATHAN ROBINS—Nineteen-year-old son of Taylor and Rebecca Robins.

LAURA, DAPHNE, DOROTHY ROBINS—Daughters of Taylor and Rebecca Robins.

MRS. BETHUNE—Served as cook for the Shieldses while they were in the Bahamas.

EDWARD DARLING—Commissioner of police in the Bahamas.

WILLIAM ST. CLAIR—An Englishman who came to a bad end in Monte Carlo.

LUCIAN BODEMAN—A native of the Bahamas who disappeared.

PARJACQUES—An inspector of police in Monte Carlo; investigated the 'cat burglar' case there.

HERR HESSELDORF AND HERR GRUNER—Germans; accompanied Pierre Dupin to Monte Carlo.

MARIE AND ANDRÉ SEBASTIAN—French husband and wife who worked for Genevieve in France.

LUCIA COMTE—A French palm reader who entertained at Genevieve's summer house.

CHARLES AROUET—A Paris police inspector.

CHARLES ATHERTON ROBINS—Grandson of English Lord Robert Atherton.

PENELOPE "PENNY" LATTIMORE—British-born; appeared at one of Genevieve's weddings.

PETER GULLY—English police sergeant.

MALCOLM TOLIVER—Inspector, New Scotland Yard, London.

The Revenge of the Robins Family

PROLOGUE

By now all the facts involved in the bizarre series of murders of the eight members of the Tyler Robins family—a case that became widely known as *Who Killed the Robins Family?*—have been established.

As mystifying as was that case, soon after was to come another series of baffling murders involving the Robins family name. Because many of the victims in the second series of murders had been connected to the deaths of the original members of the family—although not necessarily as the murderers—this case became known as *The Revenge of the Robins Family*.

It was a curious fact that in this case, too, there were

eight murders, one of which was solved at the time it happened. The other seven remain an enigma to this day.

The following pages contain an account of these eight new murders.

CHAPTER 1

INVITATION TO MURDER

THE INVITATION, ON A PLAIN WHITE card, read:

PLEASE JOIN US FOR A
MEMORIAL SERVICE
FOR THE TYLER ROBINS FAMILY
THE TIME: 2 P.M.
THE DATE: APRIL 3
THE PLACE: GREENLAWN

The words were typewritten, as were the names and addresses on the envelopes mailed out.

Later events would prove that it was this invitation that had set the stage for the first murder in the case that became known as The Revenge of the Robins Family.

Those who received the invitation of course knew the

location of Greenlawn, the sprawling estate in the Green Spring Valley of Maryland.

The estate had once belonged to Tyler Robins and his wife, Evelyn. After their deaths—and the deaths of the six Robins offspring: Marshall, James, Lewis, Libby, Cynthia, and Candace—Greenlawn had been bought and restored by the Robins family lawyer, Julian Shields, who had lived there since with his new bride, Janice.

So it was that in the early afternoon of a snowy April day, seven people, bearing invitations, began arriving at the estate.

The problem was that neither Julian nor his wife had expected visitors. They had not sent out the invitations and they were at a loss to think who might have done the deed.

Still, they tried to make the best of the awkward situation. And, in fact, they had no other real choice since by the time of the last arrival the snow had turned into an unseasonable full-blown blizzard and all the roads around Greenlawn were impassable.

"I'm afraid we're going to be snowed in for the night," Julian said philosophically, as he and Janice, assisted by the butler, Alfred Wales, and Alfred's wife, Dorina, who was the housekeeper, sought to make their visitors comfortable. There were sufficient bedrooms at Greenlawn so that arranging sleeping accommodations for the night would pose no problem although some of the guests would have to double up.

Julian was, by nature and by training—as a lawyer—a man who seldom lost his composure. Tall, slim, scholarly-looking, he was in his late fifties. At the time of these events he was president and chairman of the board of Robins Cosmetics, the other board members being the heirs of the Tyler Robins family who had originally owned and operated the multimillion-dollar business.

Julian's wife, Janice, who was British-born, was in her mid-twenties. She was also tall and slim, raven-haired, and quite lovely to look at.

On this evening Julian made a special effort to conceal his emotions because he was deeply disturbed over the matter of who had sent the invitations and what the motive might be. Could it, he wondered, be simply a harmless prank? Or was there a more sinister purpose involved?

He was led to this last thought by the fact that every one of the people who had received an invitation and had appeared at Greenlawn was somehow connected to the eight murders of the members of the Tyler Robins family.

George Pittman, who had been the first to arrive that day, had been married to one of the Robins daughters—Libby. Pittman, a stocky, broad-shouldered man, had inherited his wife's shares in Robins Cosmetics and currently served on the board of directors. He also worked as a package designer in the Robins Cosmetics laboratories in Mercer County, New Jersey, and had come to Maryland from his home in Princeton.

The next two people to present themselves at the house were Pamela Robins MacGuffin and Genevieve Robins Rollande.

Pamela had been divorced from Marshall Robins before his death. They had had one daughter, Marsha, now four years old. Because Marshall had left his money and his shares in Robins Cosmetics in trust for Marsha—to be administered by Pamela—Pamela, too, served on the company's board of directors. A still-young woman, Pamela was noticed most because of the chic fashion of her makeup and dress.

Genevieve had also been married to one of the Robins sons—James—before he was killed. She was another member of the board of directors of Robins Cosmetics since James had left her his shares in the company. Genevieve, who was a French beauty, had lived with James in Paris but had now taken up residence in New York City. Genevieve and James had a daughter, Bettina, now two years old.

Both Pamela and Genevieve had remarried a relatively short time after having been widowed. In fact, there were some people who thought they had rewed in too brief a time, and there was a flurry of gossip that perhaps both new husbands were as much fortune hunters as they were genuine suitors.

David MacGuffin, Pamela's new husband, was—curious as it may seem—a semisuccessful writer of mystery and suspense novels. He had been fascinated by the original Robins family murders and had managed to meet Pamela through mutual friends. In due course the two had been married.

Genevieve's new husband was Marc Rollande, a fellow French national, who owned an art gallery on Fifty-seventh Street in mid-Manhattan.

On this day, Pamela and Genevieve had come to Greenlawn alone, since the invitations they'd received had not included their respective spouses.

Arriving soon after the two women were Paul Bryce, Ernest Truax, and B. J. Grieg, in separate automobiles, all three brushing the snow from their hats and coats as they stood at the door before entering the house. Each carried one of the typewritten invitations.

Paul Bryce was a big-boned man with a ruddy complexion, in his early sixties. He was chairman of the board of Tiempo Cosmetics, a rival to the Robins company in the cosmetics field.

Ernest Truax, a tall, thin man of middle age, had once been employed in new-products development for Robins Cosmetics but had long since left that company and was at present employed by Paul Bryce at Tiempo Cosmetics.

To those familiar with some of the aspects of the earlier deaths of the members of the Robins family, it might have seemed odd that these two men would appear at Greenlawn on this snowy day; at one point the two of them had been accused by the now-dead Tyler Robins of stealing plans for new products from Robins Cosmetics while Ernest Truax worked there. Indeed, there had been a court case in progress some months earlier, but Julian Shields had decided to let the matter drop when he took over as president and chairman of the board of Robins Cosmetics. He gave no reason for this action.

The two men, for their part, readily admitted that they had come to Greenlawn out of curiosity after receiving invitations which they assumed had come from Julian. Both men became disconcerted when they discovered Julian had not been responsible for sending the invitations and did *not* know who had sent them. Both probably would have left immediately had it not been for the storm which now blocked their return over the roads leading away from the estate.

B. J. Grieg, on the other hand, seemed amused and intrigued by the circumstances when he found that the invitations had been sent by an anonymous party. Grieg, a stocky man of medium height, in his forties, was a private investigator who had been employed on occasion by Tyler Robins and had continued to work from time to time for Julian after the lawyer took over as head of the company.

There were three guests who *had* been expected by Julian and his wife, Janice, at Greenlawn that day. The three were Taylor Robins and Taylor's sons, Benjamin and Belden. They were the next to appear and, actually having been invited by Julian, did not of course have the typewritten invitations which had brought the others.

Taylor Robins was the deceased Tyler's brother. After Tyler Robins's death and the deaths of all the other members of his immediate family, Taylor Robins had turned up with a copy of a will which he claimed Tyler had made and sent to him.

Julian Shields had been Tyler's lawyer and he had never heard of such a will—a second will since Tyler had left everything to his wife and children in the only will the lawyer said he had seen. For months now this second will had been a point of dispute between Taylor and the others who had inherited from the original Robins family. So Julian had invited Taylor Robins to the house that day to try to settle the controversy, and Taylor Robins had brought along his two sons.

The two, in their early twenties, were twins: slender, good-looking young men who somewhat resembled Tyler's son James, who had been married to Genevieve. Twins ran in the Robins family. In Tyler's family, there had been Candace and Cynthia, identical twins except that Candace had a tiny dark mole on her left cheek. Taylor's sons, Benjamin and Belden, were also identical twins, except that Belden had a small V-shaped scar across the bridge of his nose, from a fall he had taken when he was a youngster.

It should be pointed out, in addition, that Taylor Robins, in his sixties, a large robust man with a forceful, direct manner, had been an identical twin to the late Tyler. In fact, the two looked so much alike that those who had known Tyler thought with a shock—upon seeing Taylor for the first time—that Tyler had reappeared from the dead.

When the three Robins men were in the house, Julian believed there would be no other surprise visitors that day. The snow which had continued to fall was now blinding and heaped several feet deep on the ground. And although it was still only early afternoon, the day had turned dark as night, making it necessary to turn on all the lights in the house.

Nevertheless, impassable as the roads had become, yet another person appeared, bringing one of the typewritten invitations. This person, Captain Gregory Waltham of the Maryland State Police, explained to Julian: "I had to walk the last quarter of a mile here. My car's stuck in a snowbank back just off the turnpike. Beastly day."

"Come in, Captain, come in," Julian said. "Better have a brandy to get your blood circulating. You look frozen."

Julian was surprised by the appearance of Captain Waltham but, upon reflection, realized that he should have guessed that whoever sent out the invitations would have included Waltham. The police captain had been actively involved in the investigation of the Tyler Robins family murders. In fact, recently Julian had heard rumors that the man had become slightly obsessed with trying to unravel that puzzle.

Gregory Waltham was a man of no particular physical distinction, of medium height and build and in his forties, quite ordinary looking at a glance. But these surface qualities only served to conceal an intense tenacity in Waltham's character. Impatient, demanding—of himself as well as others—he could be a formidable foe when a crime captured his interest, as the Robins family murders had done.

Julian was also surprised to see that Captain Waltham was wearing a hearing aid in his left ear. Waltham had developed a habit of lifting a hand to the ear as if to hide the appurtenance.

With Captain Waltham's arrival, there were now ten guests at Greenlawn. Only nine of them would be leaving alive.

Once Julian had seen to it that all the visitors had been assigned to various bedrooms for the night, his attention naturally turned to the curious matter of who had sent the anonymous invitations—and what the sending of them might mean. It was with this in mind that Julian, Captain Waltham, and the private detective, B. J. Grieg, met in the library while the others were upstairs.

"It's a puzzle, all right," Waltham said slowly, as he

and B. J. Grieg studied the copies of the invitation they had received.

"Then you don't think it was just a bit of mischief?" Julian asked.

Waltham shook his head. "I think not. No. It occurs to me that somebody wanted this particular group gathered together. And that what we all have in common is that we were somehow connected to the Tyler Robins family murders."

"I'm inclined to agree," Grieg said. "And if that's true, it's likely that whoever sent the notes also sent one to themselves and is here among us."

Waltham nodded again.

"Then look here now," Julian put in quickly, "if that's the case, we should try to find out as quickly as possible who that person is, as well as their motive."

The other two men once more agreed. At the suggestion of the private detective they decided it might be instructive to have everyone in the house assemble there to discuss the curious affair.

B. J. Grieg went to get a notebook from the pocket of his storm coat, which was in the bedroom he'd been assigned, and Julian left to ask Alfred to inform the guests that they were wanted in the library. Captain Waltham stayed behind, filling his pipe, lighting it, and drawing on it thoughtfully as he awaited the others.

Not long afterward Julian returned with his wife, Janice. Then Alfred came in, followed by George Pittman, Paul Bryce, Ernest Truax, Genevieve, and Pamela.

It was only then that Captain Waltham discovered Julian had not told the three Robins men that they, too, should come to the library. And, Waltham added, Dorina, the housekeeper, should also be invited to join the group. Even though none of them had received one of the anonymous invitations, it was Waltham's belief that no one present in the house that day could be eliminated as the possible perpetrator of the hoax.

Alfred left the room again, returning after a brief period with Taylor, Benjamin, and Belden Robins, followed after a time by Dorina.

Julian sat at the head of the enormous oak table in the center of the room, and the others—Captain Waltham, Genevieve, Pamela, Taylor Robins, Benjamin and Belden Robins, George Pittman, Ernest Truax, Paul Bryce, and Janice Shields—took seats in the leather armchairs around the table. Alfred and Dorina sat in chairs in the back of the room near the closed door.

Julian looked around at the group, started to speak, but broke off suddenly, asking, "Where is Mr. Grieg? Why isn't he here?"

Alfred seemed puzzled. "Sir, the last I saw of him he was here in the library with you and Captain Waltham. I hadn't noticed he wasn't in the room since."

Taylor Robins spoke up. "I saw him in a bedroom upstairs while I was on my way here."

"Well, get him, *please*!" Julian ordered Alfred.

"Yes, sir."

Alfred went to the closed door and, after twisting the knob several times, turned back toward the table, saying, "Sir, the door appears to be locked."

"Locked?" Julian asked in some bewilderment. "How can that be?"

"I don't know, sir," Alfred answered. "But it's all right."

"All right? All right?" Julian's temper was growing short.

Alfred answered quickly, "I have a duplicate key."

The butler pulled a ring of keys from his pants pocket, selected one of them, inserted it into the lock, and twisted the key back and forth.

Turning with a loud sigh, Alfred shook his head. "I can't unlock the door. It appears to have been locked from the other side by a key which is still in the lock. My key won't go in."

"You mean we've all been *locked* in this room?" Julian demanded. "What's Grieg up to?"

Alfred could only shrug.

"Is there anyone else in the house?" Captain Waltham asked.

"Not that I know of," Julian answered brusquely. "What in the world is going on here?"

"I suggest we find out at once," Waltham said. "I imagine we can go out the window and around through the front door, can't we?"

It was Alfred who answered that that was possible and who went toward one of the floor-to-ceiling windows in the front of the room. While Waltham followed Alfred, Julian went quickly to the closed library door and, thinking it might just be stuck, tried to force it open. When he found the door couldn't be budged, he hurried back across the room and followed Alfred and Captain Waltham out the open window, a flurry of snow blowing into the room. "The rest of you stay here until we get the door open," Julian told the others as he closed the window from the outside.

The snow was blinding and deep underfoot as the three men struggled their way around to the front of the house. Alfred used another of the keys from the ring in his pocket to unlock the front door and the three of them hurried inside, the butler slamming and locking the door behind them.

They immediately went to the door of the library. There was no key in the outside lock but when Julian tried the door it still wouldn't open. Alfred again used one of his keys and this time the door swung open. The others who had remained in the room were clustered around the doorway.

"I would ask that all of you stay here in the library," Julian said, "while Captain Waltham and I have a look around." His nod toward Alfred included the butler in the request.

Julian then closed the library door again and led Waltham up the stairs to the room B. J. Grieg had been assigned.

The door to this room, too, was closed. But when Julian turned the knob the door opened. The two men went inside. The body of B. J. Grieg, the private detective, was sprawled across the bed facedown. A large pair of sewing shears protruded from his back, between his shoulder blades, the shears buried in the body up to the handle. Waltham felt for a pulse. There was none.

As Julian reached out a hand toward the body, Waltham said sharply. "Don't touch anything. We must leave the room intact until the rest of my men get here."

Julian drew back, saying, "Did you notice the key there?"

There was a door key lying under the fingers of Grieg's outflung right hand on top of the bedspread.

"It did not escape my attention," Waltham said drily. "And I would be willing to wager that it fits the lock to the library door." He pointed to the sewing shears sticking into Grieg's back. "Where did those come from?"

"My wife sometimes uses this room to do her sewing," Julian said, indicating a sewing machine over in a corner.

There was a key in the inside keyhole of the room's door.

"How many keys are there to each of the rooms in the house?" the Captain asked.

"Two," Julian told him. "There should be one in each of the room's locks and Alfred has a spare for each lock."

Waltham asked Julian to get the second key to the room's lock from Alfred. He also suggested that Julian see to it that everyone waiting in the library remain there.

When Julian returned, Waltham tested both keys to see that they worked, then locked the door to the bedroom from the outside, pocketing the two keys.

The police captain and Julian then made a thorough search of the house but could find no one else there. Outside the windows the blizzard was still raging. Could some unknown person have arrived and left on foot? the captain pondered. Could that be the explanation of how Grieg had been killed after having locked all of them in the library before he died?

Waltham's next concern was to report the murder to his Maryland State Police barracks. But when he tried the phone he discovered at once that the line was dead. Either the storm had knocked out all service or someone had severed the phone lines leading to the house.

Trapped in the house by the storm and cut off from all communication, they were totally isolated from the outside world.

When Captain Waltham returned to the library he conducted a long and exhaustive interrogation of the group waiting there. He was relentless in his questioning, frequently raising a hand to his hearing aid and asking his subjects to repeat their answers. He was not unaware that this practice disconcerted them.

"Would you repeat that statement, please—and speak louder!" became his constant refrain throughout the hours of the stormy night.

Gradually, two intriguing facts emerged from this question-and-answer session. The two facts, which were connected, seemed to point to a motive for Grieg's murder.

One concerned the second will that Taylor Robins claimed his dead brother, Tyler, had left. The other fact was that Taylor Robins admitted the murdered detective had been hired by him to establish the validity of this second will.

About the second will, Taylor explained that he did not have the original document, only a duplicate. This duplicate, he went on, had been mailed to him by Tyler, along with a letter, just before Tyler went on a cruise. In the letter, still according to Taylor, his brother had written that he had made this second will to deliberately cut off Tyler's wife, Evelyn, from any inheritance. Instead, the second will left what would have been her share of the estate to Taylor.

Taylor reluctantly added that unfortunately he had since lost the letter from his brother but he could quote his brother's exact explanation for his actions: "I believe my wife, Evelyn, has found someone else and may wish to be rid of me."

Here Taylor paused before adding dramatically, "On the very cruise he took directly after sending me the letter and the will, my brother was killed and his body disposed of at sea."

Waltham frowned and asked, "And so you hired B. J. Grieg to try to locate the original copy of the second will?"

Before Taylor could answer, Julian Shields interrupted. "Captain Waltham, I'm afraid it's a bit more complicated than that. I was Tyler Robins's lawyer and I never heard of any second will. Mr. Taylor Robins here has shown me his duplicate copy of this alleged document. And not only does there seem to be no existing original but of the two witnesses whose names and signatures appear on the supposed duplicate copy, one died while Tyler Robins was on the cruise from which he never returned. That witness was an individual named Edward Birnley. He was an accountant at Robins Cosmetics. He had a heart attack."

"Yes, yes," Waltham said impatiently. "And what of the other witness?"

"According to the name and signature on the copy," Julian said quietly, "he was B. J. Grieg."

Waltham registered this piece of information with a silent nod of his head.

Taylor immediately began talking, his voice raised. Yes, it was true that Grieg had been the only living witness to the will. "But he told me he thought he could find proof that what my brother wrote about his wife was true. That's why I hired him to work for me."

The proof, Taylor went on to explain, would be found—according to the private detective—in a diary which Evelyn Robins had kept. "Mr. Grieg told me he thought that diary was somewhere here at Greenlawn and assured me he would find it. Perhaps that's why he was killed."

"Are you suggesting," Waltham asked carefully, "that it's possible Grieg locked all of us in the library so he could search the house? And that he was killed before he was able to conduct his search?"

"I said perhaps," Taylor replied.

Julian shook his head wearily, saying he thought Taylor's theory was nonsense. "For a long time now, almost everyone in this room has known about Grieg's search for Evelyn Robins's diary. At one time or another he's questioned almost all of us about it. Even Alfred. As far as I know—and I would guess as far as the others know—Evelyn's diary disappeared soon after she died. I imagine it was lost."

George Pittman, Pamela, and Genevieve readily admitted that the private detective had asked them about the diary. They all said they had no knowledge of what had become of it, and that they had told this to Grieg. Alfred added, for his part, that the private detective had phoned him several times to ask about the diary and twice had come to Greenlawn to question him about it in person.

"After Evelyn died, from a fall on an island in Greece," Julian explained, "all her belongings were shipped home, here to Greenlawn. Presumably her diary was lost at that time."

At that point, Captain Waltham ended his interrogation for the night, no closer to the truth of why Grieg was killed nor of who might have murdered him than he had been when the body had been discovered.

Nor did Waltham have any idea of who had sent the anonymous invitations that day which had brought them together at Greenlawn. Any one of the persons present might have been the anonymous party. Even, Waltham thought, B. J. Grieg.

And if the private detective *had* been killed to prevent him from finding the diary and so establishing the validity of a second will—well, once again, there were sure to be plenty of suspects. Anyone who benefited by actions Evelyn had taken—before her death—*because she had been included in her husband's will*—would be affected if that will were superseded by a second will.

As the group that had been assembled in the library left the room to go to the bedrooms on the upper floors, they were suddenly startled by the sound of a loud knocking on the outside of the front door.

"Who in the world can that be?" Julian exclaimed, puzzled.

Dorina ran forward a few paces, saying, "Oh, maybe it's Carrie and Molly."

The group paused where they were while Julian went to the door and opened it.

A whirlwind of snow blew into the hallway, followed by a man covered with snow from the crown of his hat to the tips of his rubber boots. It took him several seconds to brush the snow away enough so that the others could see that he was Marc Rollande, Genevieve's husband.

"Marc!" Genevieve cried out and ran to him.

Marc Rollande was a muscular man with black wavy hair, dark-skinned face, and a black mustache.

Once Rollande had shed his coat, hat, and boots, and had warmed himself, he explained that he had hoped to surprise Genevieve. He had flown to Baltimore earlier in the day, rented a car, and set out for the Green Spring Valley only to be caught in the blizzard. He had had to abandon the car some miles away and make the rest of the trip on foot. Shaking his head, he admitted that several times on the way there he was certain he was lost and would end up frozen to death. But finally he had made it.

"It was a foolish thing to do," he added sheepishly.

After Rollande had told his story, Captain Waltham, curious, asked Dorina, "When we heard the knocking on the door, you said something about 'maybe it's Carrie.' What did you mean? Who's Carrie?"

Alfred explained, for his wife, that Carrie was their daughter, who also lived at Greenlawn. That day Carrie and her daughter, Molly, had gone shopping in Baltimore. Both Alfred and Dorina assumed that the daughter and her child had remained in the city once the storm had started. But since all the telephones were out, they couldn't be sure of this. And so, when Dorina had heard someone at the door, she had thought it might be Carrie.

That ended the events for this strange and stormy

day and evening at Greenlawn and soon afterward everyone in the house went to bed while outside the blizzard still howled.

The next morning the storm had ended and the sky was clear with a bright sun that struck shafts of glittering light off the mountains of snow rising high everywhere outside the house.

Captain Waltham hailed the first snowplow to appear and dispatched it back to summon members of the Maryland State Police homicide team to the estate.

When the forensic squad and the medical examiner arrived, they went to work on the room where the murder had occurred. They were unable to come up with any clues or information that would help the investigation. The death of B. J. Grieg, according to the medical examiner, was caused by stab wounds inflicted by the sewing shears. The key found under the dead man's hand in the bedroom *did* fit the lock to the library door.

Later in the morning, while the police were still on the scene, Carrie, the daughter of Alfred and Dorina Wales, returned to Greenlawn with her child, Molly. Captain Waltham, simply as a precautionary measure, had a check made on Carrie's whereabouts the previous night. Police were able to confirm that, as she had told them, she had been in a hotel in Baltimore on the day and evening in question.

At midday Marc Rollande—with the help of a snowplow—managed to uncover his car a couple of miles away from the estate.

Although the police stayed on at Greenlawn most of that day, questioning those present and searching the house and grounds for clues, no real evidence was turned up to help solve the murder. They were, however, able to determine that the phone lines outside the house had been severed, which explained why it had been impossible to make any calls into or from the estate.

In subsequent days, under the direction of Captain Waltham, the continuing police investigation slowly amassed a body of information about the dead man, B. J. Grieg, and those who might be considered suspects in the case.

Here it should be remarked that Gregory Waltham was an old-fashioned cop in several respects. Thus, although he sometimes used modern technological equipment, such as computers, to help him in his work, he also employed other, more simple methods to enable him to sort out his thoughts. One of these methods was to jot down information, as he received it, on a set of three by five file cards. He would then review the cards periodically, trying to fit the bits of information together, like pieces of a puzzle.

In the investigation into the background of B. J. Grieg, police discovered from an examination of the bank account of the murdered private eye that he had been making regular deposits of substantial amounts of money. When police checked Grieg's own business records, there appeared to be no explanation for the source of these deposits.

On one of the three by five cards, Captain Waltham noted:

> *B. J. Grieg:*
> *Hired by Taylor Robins to find original copy*

of 2nd Tyler Robins will and diary of Evelyn Robins. Also did work for Julian Shields and Robins Cosmetics from time to time. Conflict of interest? Made large bank deposits, no explanation for source of this money. Blackmail? Who? Why?

In the instances of others who might be considered suspects in the murder of B. J. Grieg, the continuing investigation elicited certain facts that Captain Waltham had been unable to uncover during his interrogation at Greenlawn on the night the private eye was killed. These facts might or might not have had a bearing on the case.

There was, for example, the matter of a possible attempt by others to take over Robins Cosmetics. Julian Shields and the other members of the board of the company were aware of this possibility, Captain Waltham discovered.

"I don't think it has anything to do with the murder," Julian told police, "but we have heard rumors that there may be a move afoot by outsiders to try to gain a controlling interest in the company."

When Waltham pressed him in the matter, Julian added that he had heard Paul Bryce and Taylor Robins were behind the plan. "But I do not know this for a fact." In answer to further questioning by the captain, Julian said that, yes, the other members of the board had been advised of these rumors.

Paul Bryce, for his part, when questioned by Captain Waltham, would neither admit nor deny having any interest in acquiring Robins Cosmetics and merging it with his own company, Tiempo Cosmetics. "Since I think that a business matter such as you suggest, whether true or not, is hardly the concern of the police, I have no comment. I might add that I have been advised by my lawyer that the answer I have just given you is the proper one."

Taylor Robins, on the other hand, willingly admitted to Waltham that he intended to become a part of Robins Cosmetics, although he, too, would not say directly that it would be through an attempted stock takeover of the company.

"It galls me," Taylor Robins said, "that my brother built a company called Robins Cosmetics and yet there is at present not one person by that name anywhere on the board of directors. Yes, sir, I do mean to take steps to remedy that situation."

Waltham duly noted the information he'd acquired on additional three by five cards:

Julian Shields:

Worried about possible takeover of company. Could Grieg's search for a 2nd will and the diary have threatened Shields? Could Shields himself, planning to kill Grieg, have sent the anonymous invitations so there would be plenty of possible suspects present at the time of the murder? Shields, who did not inherit any Robins stock, was made chairman of company by Evelyn Robins before her death and has remained chairman by consent of other board members. He would seem to have the most to lose if the company was taken over by outsiders.

* * *

Paul Bryce:

Has always been a tough Robins Cosmetics competitor. Would undoubtedly like to acquire company. Why did he and Ernest Truax receive invitations to estate? If Grieg, bent on some underhanded plan of his own, sent the anonymous invitations—and included Bryce—could Bryce have been victim of Grieg's blackmail scheme?

Taylor Robins:

Likely suspect. Very arrogant. Determined to wrest his way into company. Has built his own empire in communications, radio and TV stations, and newspapers in Chicago but is clearly a man for whom there is never enough power. Also probably had a sibling rivalry with his twin brother, Tyler, wants to get his hands on company Tyler built before Tyler died. Business of 2nd will sounds suspiciously fishy. Curious business about his relationship with Grieg. Could he have been victim of Grieg's blackmail?

And, finally, based on information Waltham had come by through the continuing investigation, he added yet another three by five card to his file:

Evelyn Robins's Diary:

Virtually every person questioned has verified existence of diary. Last known to have been with her on island in Greece. No one admits to having seen it since. Was Grieg's search for diary really the motive for his murder? Taylor Robins makes a big case for the importance of the diary—BUT—could it be only a red herring?

It was at this point in the investigation that Captain Gregory Waltham was summoned to the office of the chief inspector, commander of the Maryland State Police barracks. There, Waltham was ordered to be in court in Baltimore to testify in an earlier, unrelated homicide case, a case that was expected to take several weeks to complete.

For the time being the murder of B. J. Grieg remained unsolved.

CHAPTER 2

DEAD ON TARGET

IT IS UNFORTUNATE THAT CAPTAIN Gregory Waltham was far from the scene when the next murder in the series of grisly deaths took place, that scene being the Bahamas and Waltham being still in court in Baltimore.

Not long after the death of B. J. Grieg at Greenlawn, Julian Shields had decided that a change of scene was in order. He had chosen a trip to the Bahamas because it would enable him and Janice and the board members of Robins Cosmetics to combine pleasure with business.

For some time now Genevieve's husband, Marc Rollande, had been urging the board of directors to invest some of the company's profits in a new bank which was soon to open in the Bahamas. The man behind the new bank, Pierre Dupin, was a Frenchman who had been a friend of Rollande's in Paris. Julian was against the move but some of the board members, especially George Pittman, favored the action. Julian finally made a decision to have a meeting between Dupin and the others in the Bahamas to settle the matter once and for all.

Julian had arranged to rent a villa on one of the islands, complete with small guest cottages. He and Janice stayed in the villa itself while the others occupied the cottages. Pamela and her mystery-writer husband, David MacGuffin, were in one cottage, Genevieve and her husband, Marc, in another, George Pittman, alone, in a third cottage, and Alfred, alone, in the remaining one. Julian had wanted Alfred along on the trip because the butler was accustomed to serving them wherever they were, but Alfred's wife, Dorina, had stayed behind at Greenlawn.

The villa and cottages sat high on a lush green hillside overlooking the sea and miles of sandy beach. Everywhere around them the land was ablaze with vivid colors—plants, flowers, and houses—as if all of them had been colored by a set of children's crayons. The group took pleasure in the exotic surroundings and the sea, especially Julian and George Pittman who spent most of their spare time scuba diving. George preferred the early morning while Julian chose the late afternoon.

For Julian, the only real cloud on the horizon was the presence of Taylor Robins and Taylor's family who had come to the Bahamas on a yacht, which remained anchored offshore not far from the villa. Julian couldn't be sure who in his group had tipped off Taylor that the board members of Robins Cosmetics would be there, but he suspected that George Pittman was the culprit. Julian also had no doubt that the reason Taylor Robins had appeared in the Bahamas was because he wanted to keep an eye on what the board members were doing. Furthermore, Julian was almost certain that George would be making regular reports to Taylor about the affairs of Robins Cosmetics.

For some time now Julian had been growing increasingly aware that George Pittman would like to oust him, Julian, as chairman of Robins Cosmetics. Thus he could easily believe that George would do all he could to aid Taylor in a possible takeover of the company.

From the time the Taylor Robins family arrived on the scene, they slept aboard the yacht instead of taking quarters on the island. Still, they were such frequent visitors at the villa that sometimes Julian felt they might as well have moved in.

On this trip Taylor Robins had brought along his entire family. The family included not only the twins, Benjamin and Belden, but Taylor's wife, Rebecca, and their other four grown offspring.

Rebecca Robins at fifty-nine—three years younger than her husband—was a comely woman who had taken great care with her health and looks.

Jonathan, the other Robins son, was the last-born of the children, nineteen now, four years younger than his twin brothers.

The three daughters ranged in age from twenty to twenty-seven. Laura was the youngest girl, Daphne was twenty-five, and Dorothy, twenty-seven, was the eldest of the children. They all worked in some part of their father's communications empire in Chicago, Benjamin and Belden at a TV station, Jonathan at a newspaper,

Laura and Daphne at a radio station, and Dorothy at a magazine. Only Dorothy had married, a marriage that had ended in divorce some years earlier.

With all these Robinses around all the time at the villa, Julian found it difficult to ignore them. Especially since all the people Julian had invited to the Bahamas seemed to enjoy their company so much. Even Janice, who was usually so solicitous of Julian's every feeling, remarked to him: "They're such a charming group. And so thoughtful. Every time one of them appears here at the villa, they bring a present."

Julian simply smiled and did not attempt to answer with what he thought was the truth: that the Robinses were making a calculated effort to ingratiate themselves.

On the other hand, Julian was withholding judgment at the way things were going in the discussions he and the board members were having with Pierre Dupin, who hoped to get them to invest Robins Cosmetics money in Dupin's new bank.

Julian had had misgivings about the project from the first time Marc Rollande had proposed it. Now, after a couple of meetings with Dupin, Julian had become even more wary. Julian sized Dupin up as a shrewd manipulator. And although the possibility was never mentioned in any of the meetings, Julian became increasingly convinced that Dupin meant to use the bank for "washing" illicit money. None of the other board members brought the matter up in private conversations, but Julian could sense an uneasiness among them, even on the part of George Pittman. Marc Rollande—who was not a board member, but did have considerable influence on his wife, Genevieve, who was—continued to urge the group to invest in the bank. Julian decided to wait until after a few more meetings with Dupin before taking a board vote.

At this time there occurred an event which was to change all their pleasure and business plans in the Bahamas.

As has been noted earlier, Dorina Wales, the regular cook-housekeeper, did not accompany the group on the trip. In her place, Julian and Janice had hired a local woman—Mrs. Bethune was her name—to cook for them while they were there. She was an excellent choice and they all enjoyed her dishes. It became a morning ritual for all the group, and sometimes members of the Robins family as well, to gather at the villa for a breakfast cooked by Mrs. Bethune and served by Alfred. The time for the meal each day was 8 A.M. and George Pittman, having gone scuba diving earlier, was always the last one to arrive at the table.

On the sixth morning that they had been there, they all were gathered and waiting—including Taylor and Rebecca who had come from the yacht—when Mrs. Bethune came in from the kitchen to announce that Alfred had failed to appear to serve them.

"That's odd," Julian said. "Not like him at all. Always prompt. I wonder if he's ill? I'd better go have a look."

David MacGuffin, Pamela's husband, suggested that he go along with Julian. The others remained at breakfast, Janice and Genevieve and Pamela volunteering to serve the meal.

David MacGuffin wore his sandy hair styled in a shaggy cut and his glasses were horn-rimmed, both effects chosen to give him—for the photograph on the jackets of his books—what he hoped was the appearance of a writer. This effort, like most of the mystery novels he wrote, did not quite succeed.

The cottage Alfred occupied was several yards removed from the villa and it took the two men a few minutes to cover the distance. When they reached the cottage, Julian knocked on the door several times and, when there was no answer, tried the doorknob and found the door was unlocked. The two men went inside.

The cottage was quite small, consisting of a living room, bedroom, and bath. As soon as Julian, who was in the lead, stepped into the living room, he paused and exclaimed, "Something's dreadfully wrong here!"

"Oh, yes," MacGuffin replied.

At first the men could see only that the inside of the cottage had been thoroughly ransacked, with desk, table, and dresser drawers pulled out and their contents dumped on the floor. Pillows from the sofa and two chairs had been slashed open and piled atop each other, and Alfred's clothes, torn and slashed and left in a heap on the floor.

Moving gingerly through the three rooms, the men made a second, more sinister, discovery in the bathroom. There, on the tile floor, was a smear of blood and a smashed whiskey bottle. There was blood on the jagged glass edges of the broken bottle and stuck in the blood were what looked like human hairs.

"Do you suppose. . . ?" MacGuffin whispered and couldn't finish the sentence. As a writer of murder mysteries MacGuffin had often created scenes of extreme violence but now, faced with the real situation, he felt quite faint.

"I don't know what to suppose," Julian answered vaguely, "but what I think we should do is get back to the house at once and summon the authorities."

Within a very short time the police arrived at the villa, led by the commissioner of police, a man named Edward Darling, who was dressed in a dark blue uniform resplendent with insignia and silver buttons.

After talking with Julian and MacGuffin at the villa, Darling and his men quickly headed toward the cottage Alfred had occupied, followed by Julian and MacGuffin.

"And this is exactly the way you found the place?" the commissioner inquired after surveying the scene inside. "You didn't touch anything?"

"Nothing, no," Julian said quickly. "Everything looked just like this. We didn't touch a thing."

Commissioner Darling nodded and then set his men to work searching the cottage and the grounds for possible clues. Julian and MacGuffin stayed back out of the way.

Some time passed before the police concluded that phase of their investigation. From the cottage they took the smashed bottle with the blood-encrusted hairs on it and a comb and brush which presumably held hairs from Alfred's head. To the naked eye the hairs on the smashed bottle appeared to match those in the comb and brush. Also, in the bathroom medicine cabinet the police spotted a straight-edged razor with traces of blood on it, and they took the razor along with them.

"It's possible that the victim accidentally nicked himself while shaving with his razor," Commissioner Darling observed. "But on the other hand, the razor has been carefully wiped clean of all fingerprints." He shook his head and added, "As has every other surface in the place."

The police did make what they considered one significant find outside the cottage. From the beach, at the edge of the sea, they recovered a single shoe lying on its side in the sand. There were what looked like traces of blood across the tip of the shoe. Julian was able to identify the shoe as looking like one of a pair worn by Alfred.

The commissioner then accompanied Julian and MacGuffin back to the villa where the others who had been there that morning had stayed. Commissioner Darling, assisted by a police sergeant, spent the next several hours interrogating the group. No one seemed able to provide any information that would help the investigation.

The commissioner saved his most rigorous grilling for George Pittman, because Pittman had been the last one to appear for breakfast that morning.

"I told you," George Pittman finally said in exasperation, "that the reason I was late was because I went scuba diving."

"But no one saw you," the commissioner pointed out. "We have only your word for that."

George shook his head wearily. "No, no one saw me, I assume. But I've been skin diving every morning since we've been here. And the last one to breakfast every morning. Nothing happened to Alfred on any of those other mornings. Why should you think I had anything to do with what happened *this* morning?"

"Ah, you have a point there, Mr. Pittman," Darling conceded, smiling faintly.

"Besides," George went on, "why wouldn't you suspect first of all that this was a robbery by some outsider. It certainly looks that way."

The commissioner nodded. "Perhaps."

"I have a question, Commissioner," Julian interjected. "I couldn't help but notice that when you were questioning each of us in turn, you put special emphasis on whether any one of us had heard a disturbance in the night. What makes you think it happened during the night?"

Darling again smiled faintly. "The shoe. Finding it on the beach at the edge of the water the way we did would indicate that if somebody took the body down and dumped it into the surf and the shoe fell off," he spread his hands in the air, "it would not have been noticed in the darkness."

The commissioner paused, raised his eyebrows, and added, "Or perhaps someone wanted us to think that."

Julian and the others would have liked nothing better than to pack up and go home at that point. But the police requested that they remain temporarily and so they felt they had no choice but to delay their departure.

Taylor Robins and his family did not escape questioning by the police either, because Commissioner Darling had ascertained that they, too, had some connection with Alfred Wales. So, though they were not able to give any answers to the police questions, they also were requested to remain temporarily.

Meanwhile, Julian had to phone Dorina, Alfred's wife, in Maryland and inform her of what had happened. She flew to the Bahamas that same day, expressing shock and bewilderment when she arrived. Julian, Janice, and the others attempted to comfort her as best they could. When the police questioned her as to who might have killed her husband, or why, she had no answer for them.

It took a while longer before Commissioner Darling and his men—working with the police in Maryland—were positively able to determine that the blood found on the smashed bottle was the same blood type as Alfred Wales's and so was the blood on the straight razor. And that the hairs on the bottle also matched Alfred Wales's hairs found on the comb and brush in the cottage, as well as other hairs taken from a second comb and brush belonging to Alfred which was at the estate in Maryland.

There the case rested, inconclusive. Much as Commissioner Darling regretted it, he knew he could not expect the group to remain indefinitely and so the day came when he decided to tell them they were free to leave. He drove out to the villa.

"I'm very much relieved to hear that," Julian said when he was informed by Darling.

Breakfast was again being served at the villa and Julian, expansively, asked the commissioner to join the meal.

Before the commissioner could reply there came a loud cry from the grounds outside the villa. The words carried quite clearly through one of the open windows: "Help! Somebody come quick! *He's been murdered!*"

"What—?" Commissioner Darling started to say.

Julian cut in quickly. "That's Dorina's voice! She's been at one of the cottages, packing up her husband's belongings."

The commissioner and the two policemen who had come with him to the villa hurried outside, the others who had been at the table close on their heels. On this particular morning none of the Robinses had come over from the yacht, so the group trailing behind out of the house included Julian, Janice, Pamela and David MacGuffin, Genevieve and Marc Rollande, and the cook, Mrs. Bethune.

Dorina Wales stood not far from the beach, still shouting hysterically. Commissioner Darling was the first one to reach her and he took her by the arm, saying, "See here, what's this all about?"

Dorina pointed to the edge of the beach. "There! There! See there!"

They all looked in the direction to which she was pointing. And then they saw the body lying on the sand at water's edge.

Once again the commissioner led the way until he was within a yard or so of the body. He then made a motion with his arm, shouting an order to the others following him: "Stay back now till I have a close look at this."

Darling approached the body gingerly, watching the sand underfoot and circling around when he got near the spot where the body lay. The others, waiting back out of the way as they'd been ordered, could clearly see what was going on.

It was George Pittman who lay on the sand. He was wearing a scuba-diving suit and goggles. He had been gut-shot by a spear gun, the sleek metal projectile protruding from his body front and back.

"He's quite dead," the commissioner of police announced. He then pointed to a strip of sand between the body and the spot where the group was standing. "Footprints," he said and the others could make them out in the wet sand, two sets of prints, side by side, which had been left by rubber fins. The footprints led down the beach toward the body and then a few paces on and into the surf, as if the two people who had left them had continued on into the sea, and not returned up the beach. A spear gun lay on the sand near the footprints.

"Get some lab people here at once," the commissioner ordered one of the policemen. "I want casts made of these prints before the tide comes in. And get the coroner out here, too."

"Yes, sir," one of the policemen answered quickly and started back toward the villa, Janice, Genevieve, Pamela, and Mrs. Bethune going along with him.

Commissioner Darling quickly questioned Dorina about finding the body.

The poor woman could hardly gasp out the words as she explained that she had left the cottage where she had been packing up her late husband's clothes and was on her way to the villa when she spotted the body. "He was stretched out there just as you see him now," she said. "I took one look and started screaming."

The commissioner frowned. "And that's all you saw?"

Dorina nodded. "That's all I saw. Can I go now?"

Darling dismissed her and she hurried off toward the villa.

"Which cottage was Mr. Pittman staying in?" the commissioner asked Julian. Julian indicated the building.

Leaving the other policemen to stand guard over the

body, Darling, Julian, David MacGuffin, and Marc Rollande went to George Pittman's cottage.

As soon as the men stepped inside, they saw that the scene was almost identical to the scene they'd observed in the cottage Alfred Wales had occupied, with papers, clothes, cushions scattered everywhere, drawers yanked open, chairs and tables overturned.

"Looks like the same person who ransacked Alfred's place did the job here," MacGuffin said.

Commissioner Darling grunted, and mumbled something under his breath.

They were joined then by the policeman who had gone to the villa to phone for additional help. Commissioner Darling left this policeman at the cottage while he, Julian, MacGuffin, and Marc Rollande returned to the villa.

There, Darling once again put everyone through an interrogation. And once again no one seemed to have any satisfactory information about this latest murder in their midst.

"Let me ask you this," the police commissioner said, glancing around at the assembled group. "Can any one of you think of a reason why anyone would have wanted to get these two men, Alfred Wales and George Pittman, out of the way so they could search their cottages?"

Julian spoke up, choosing his words carefully as he explained that there *had* been some talk about a missing diary. He told the commissioner all about the occurrences at Greenlawn when B. J. Grieg was killed and that there had been talk then of a diary. Julian concluded by adding, "There's no proof that either of them had the diary or that the diary is what this is all about. But you did ask and that's the only thing I can think of that has ever been mentioned."

Darling had no further questions of them but he now decided he wanted to question Taylor Robins since Taylor was the one who had been seeking the diary.

For the next two days the police were busy searching the cottages and the beach and grounds for possible clues. They found none. An autopsy performed on George Pittman revealed no unexpected facts. He had died as a result of the wound from the spear gun. There were no prints on the spear gun.

Taylor Robins, when questioned by Commissioner Darling, did have some answers that were new but they did as much to deepen the two mysteries as to help clear them up.

According to Taylor Robins, George Pittman *had* approached him in the Bahamas, saying that it was possible that he, George Pittman, might be able to produce the long-lost diary kept by Evelyn Robins—for a price.

Taylor claimed that Pittman was very evasive about where the diary was but suggested that if they could make a deal, perhaps the diary could be turned over to Taylor. The deal Pittman wanted was for Taylor to gain control, one way or another, of Robins Cosmetics and for him, George Pittman, to be made chairman. Taylor claimed that he told Pittman he'd need more proof that Pittman could actually get the diary for him. They set a date to talk again, the date being the very night of the morning Pittman was found dead.

When Taylor was asked if anyone else was present during his conversation with Pittman, Taylor said no but that the two of them had had their talk at the villa and that as they were completing their conversation, Alfred had appeared to serve them drinks. Upon reflection, Taylor said, it now occurred to him that Pittman had seemed a bit unsettled when Alfred had appeared. Or perhaps, Taylor concluded, that had been only his own imagination.

There was one other development in the case. A day before they all departed from the Bahamas, the police completed an analysis of the prints left in the wet sand near George Pittman's body. According to their calculations, whoever left the two pairs of prints were almost identical in weight and stride.

The following day, Julian and his group and the Taylor Robins family left the Bahamas, the former taking with them the body of George Pittman. The matter of whether or not Robins Cosmetics would invest any money in the bank that Marc Rollande's friend, Pierre Dupin, planned to open in the Bahamas was left unresolved, much to Julian's relief, and to Rollande's chagrin.

A few days later George Pittman was buried in the Robins family plot at a small cemetery in the Green Spring Valley of Maryland, not far from the Greenlawn estate.

With George Pittman dead, the board of directors of Robins Cosmetics needed a new member. David MacGuffin, Pamela's husband, was unanimously elected to fill the vacancy.

CHAPTER 3

A FATAL IMPERSONATION

JULIAN SHIELDS HAD NOT WANTED TO go to Monte Carlo when he and Janice were invited there for a holiday by Taylor Robins. But that's where the lawyer, his wife with him, found himself approximately one month after the burial of George Pittman in Maryland.

Julian felt he had no choice but to accept the invitation after he discovered that Genevieve and Marc Rollande and Pamela and David MacGuffin had also been invited and were going. Knowing as he did that Taylor still wanted to take over Robins Cosmetics, Julian felt that he himself could ill afford to let so many members of the board of directors of the company spend time with Taylor without being there himself.

The lawyer also suspected that Taylor had a possible additional ulterior motive for inviting the group of them to Monte Carlo. Ever since they had all been together, first at Greenlawn during the snowstorm and later in the Bahamas, it had become increasingly apparent that one of the Robins twins, Belden, and Genevieve had become very much attracted to one another. This, despite the fact that Genevieve was still very much married to Marc Rollande. Julian guessed that Genevieve was, perhaps fatally, attracted to Belden because that young man so much resembled his now-dead cousin, James, whom Genevieve had loved deeply during her marriage to him.

Julian was concerned about this situation. Not only did he worry that Marc, who had a violent temper, would catch on to what was transpiring between the two—and that there could be some unpleasant fireworks as a result—but also that Taylor was attempting to further the affair. Julian believed that Taylor would like nothing better than to have Belden break up the marriage of Genevieve and Marc, and then marry her, as another attempt by Taylor to worm his or his family's way into Robins Cosmetics.

So it was with a great sense of unease that Julian made the trip to Monte Carlo.

Taylor Robins had spared no expense in arranging for the holiday they all were to spend. He had taken over an entire floor in the hotel to house them—a hotel overlooking the Mediterranean, with a gambling casino on the first floor. To add to their pleasure, Taylor had had his yacht brought to Monte Carlo and anchored just offshore for cruises up and down the coast.

"I want you to enjoy yourselves as my guests," Taylor announced to them the first day the entire group was together and had met for a welcoming champagne party on the Robins yacht. "Let's forget about past unpleasantness and about all our business affairs and have a carefree holiday."

For the next several days, Taylor appeared true to his word about making the occasion nothing more than a holiday; never once did he broach the subject of the second will, the lost diary, or Robins Cosmetics.

Almost every day they all went out on the yacht, although some days the women went shopping together, and every evening the group changed into gowns and black tie and went gambling in the casino. Julian, Taylor, and Marc Rollande were particularly lucky at roulette, walking away with winnings each night. And the others also won frequently enough to keep them coming back with eager anticipation. There was an undeniable excitement for all of them at being in such a glamorous setting.

To add further spice to the adventure, the second day they were there the whole of Monte Carlo was abuzz with the news that there was a jewel thief at work in the municipality. A "cat burglar" the police and press called the thief who climbed in through windows in the middle of the night and made off with jewelry and other valuables while most of his victims slept unsuspectingly.

The burglar had not gotten away unseen every time, however. Twice the targets of his robberies had awakened while he was still in the room. Both times the victims had been women alone and both times when the women had attempted to cry out, the thief had pounced upon them and gagged them with delicate silk scarves to quiet them, then bound them with strips of bedsheet.

Both women had described the thief as wearing a

black turtleneck sweater, black knit cap, and a stocking mask. They both stated that, despite the circumstances, he "acted gentlemanly." The only other clues the police had were that the scarves were identical and that both scarves gave off a pleasant, slightly astringent scent. The fact that he entered and left the scenes of his crimes through windows on high floors of the buildings had earned him his nickname.

When the news first circulated that a cat burglar was on the prowl, most people found it only added a hint of glamorous danger to the already exotic setting.

Frequently, when Julian, Taylor, and the others in their group were leaving the casino for the night to go to their rooms, one or another of the women would warn jokingly, "Watch out for the cat burglar."

The next time the thief struck, the situation grew more ominous. Twice in a single evening the cat burglar struck, robbed his victims, and escaped. This time there was a difference, though; the thief, in leaving his two female victims gagged, had caused them—through carelessness perhaps, perhaps deliberately—to suffocate.

Meanwhile, about this same time, a further bit of unpleasantness entered the lives of Julian and his group and the Robins family with the arrival on the scene of Pierre Dupin, from the Bahamas. Dupin, accompanied by two burly, stone-faced men who appeared to be his bodyguards, checked into the same hotel where the group was staying.

The unpleasantness came from the fact that Dupin, alone or with his escorts, was observed in heated discussions with Marc Rollande upon more than one occasion.

It seemed clear that Dupin was pressuring Rollande over some matter, probably having to do with raising money for the bank in the Bahamas, Julian secretly surmised.

Rollande, for his part, turned surly with everyone around him, began drinking heavily day and night, and also began to gamble recklessly at the roulette table where he invariably lost.

Julian believed that all his own worst fears were about to be realized, especially since Genevieve, Rollande's wife, was now openly showing her real affection and preference for Belden Robins, the two of them more often than not slipping away furtively for two or three hours at a time. Despite Julian's anxiety, Marc Rollande did not seem to notice the goings-on between his wife and Belden, or chose to ignore them.

In addition to everything else that was transpiring, there came a piece of puzzling news from the police in the Bahamas which might or might not have had a bearing on the events that had happened there.

Julian received a telephone call from Commissioner of Police Edward Darling. Darling reported that his men, continuing to investigate and question all persons on the island known to have been arrested in the past for robberies or crimes of violence, had discovered that one such man had disappeared, along with his fishing boat.

"I don't know whether he had anything to do with what happened out at your villa," the commissioner of police reported, "but we have received a report from the police in Miami, Florida, that this man's boat was found abandoned offshore there. There was no sign of the man. His name, incidentally, was Lucian Bodeman. A bad character. Ever hear the name?"

"No," Julian said.

"Well," Darling concluded, "I just wanted you to know what we know. And to assure you that we're continuing the investigation. I'll keep you informed."

"Thank you, Commissioner," Julian said.

Later, when Julian told the others who had been in the Bahamas of this news, none of them could recall ever having heard the man's name.

On the night before the holiday in Monte Carlo was to end—and to Julian's vast relief there had been no scandalous scene between Marc Rollande and Genevieve, after all—there was an elaborate masked ball in the courtyard of the hotel. They all were invited to attend and the women in the group made elaborate preparations for the gowns they planned to wear. The men would go in black tie and, as a concession to the idea of the ball, would wear simple black eye masks which the hotel supplied.

There was an orchestra set up in the courtyard and Japanese lanterns strung around the dance floor, under the open, starlit sky. White-jacketed waiters moved through and around the crowd, carrying trays of bubbling champagne.

Julian, dancing with one or another of the women in the group and enjoying himself, nevertheless tried to keep an eye on Genevieve and Belden. Marc Rollande had not yet appeared in the courtyard and Julian was hopeful that they all might get through the evening without an incident.

At one point when Julian noticed that Genevieve and Belden seemed to be dancing together every dance, he crossed and cut in on Belden, sweeping Genevieve away, whispering into her ear, "My dear, it's none of my business, I know, but must you dance every dance with Belden? I'm only concerned—"

"Julian, Julian, Julian," Genevieve interrupted. "That wasn't Belden I was dancing with. That was Benjamin!"

Julian came to a standstill. "Are you sure?"

"Of course," Genevieve answered, laughing. "You hadn't yet arrived when the twins announced to everyone present how they could be identified tonight. Belden is wearing a red carnation in the lapel of his dinner jacket." She turned Julian so he could see the man who had been dancing with her. He was dancing with Rebecca Robins. He had no red carnation in his lapel. "That's Benjamin," Genevieve said. She turned Julian again. "That's Belden dancing with your wife." Julian saw the red carnation in Belden's lapel.

The orchestra came to the end of the number before they could begin dancing again. Genevieve linked her arm through Julian's and as they started to walk across the floor, a waiter approached and said to Genevieve, "Madame Rollande?"

"Yes?" Genevieve asked, puzzled.

"Your husband, Monsieur Rollande, asks if you could please come up to your room for a moment," the waiter said.

"Of course."

Before she could leave, Belden and Janice strolled over. Genevieve explained that Marc wanted to see her in their room and the orchestra began to play again. Janice said that she had promised this dance to David MacGuffin.

"And you promised *me* this dance," Belden protested

to Genevieve. "This is one of my favorite numbers. Marc can wait a few more minutes."

She agreed. Belden insisted that he would escort Janice over to MacGuffin, and Genevieve promised she'd wait. Julian simply raised his eyebrows and then stood with Genevieve watching Belden and Janice disappear through the crowd of dancers. Julian asked Genevieve if she wanted to dance with him until Belden returned.

"Oh, here's Belden now," Genevieve said and moved away.

Julian watched the two of them melt into each other's arms, after she had paused to straighten the red carnation in his lapel, and dance away. Julian sighed and took a glass of champagne from the tray of a passing waiter. But he continued to be uneasy, anticipating the appearance of Marc Rollande, fearing that Rollande would now really be enraged that Genevieve had not come to the room.

When the orchestra finished the number they'd been playing and went directly into another number, and Genevieve and Belden continued to dance together, Julian decided to act. He went quickly over and said, "Now look here—"

Before he could finish his words, there came a shrill, piercing scream from out in the center of the dance floor: "Look! Look! Oh!" The orchestra music died away slowly.

The cry was picked up all over the courtyard and people everywhere were pointing upward. It took Julian several seconds to focus his eyes upward and spot the focus for the cries of alarm.

High up over the courtyard in the clearly lighted

frame of an open window on the fourth or fifth floor of the hotel was a figure leaning backward out of the window. From what could be seen the figure was clad in black and seemed to be struggling with an unseen figure inside the room.

Then, as the crowd watched in horrified silence, the figure tumbled outward slowly and fell, almost as if in slow motion, downward, the body turning over and over in the air until it hit with a sickening thud on the hard concrete surface of the courtyard, well away from where the crowd stood.

Part of the crowd scattered backward from where the body lay, while another part surged forward for a better look. Julian, caught up among those who pressed forward, let himself be carried along.

Someone in the forefront of the crowd now standing in a circle around the body said loudly, "It's the cat burglar!"

Julian could see that the figure lying on the surface of the courtyard was clad in a black turtleneck sweater, black slacks, dark canvas shoes, black knit cap, and a stocking mask which distorted the features of the face so that the face was grotesquely shapeless.

Another voice in the crowd called out: "Let me through. I'm a doctor."

Then the doctor was bending over the inert body, checking for life signs before pronouncing, "He's dead. Quite dead."

The manager of the hotel was the next one to push his way through, saying, "Stand back now. Don't anyone touch the body. The police have been called."

Although the police were a long while in arriving, few

of the people in the courtyard left. And as word spread through the hotel of what had happened, more people who had been inside gambling at the casino came out and joined the onlookers. The excitement of finding the cat burglar dead there in the courtyard swept through the assemblage like an electrical shock.

There were six police officers who had responded to the call and for a time they, too, simply stood looking down at the dead man until their superior, an inspector of police, got there.

Julian, who had remained where he was, had been joined by Taylor Robins, Belden and Benjamin, and MacGuffin. The women had stayed in the background, out of viewing distance of the corpse.

The inspector of police, Parjacques, spoke briefly with the doctor who had examined the body and with the hotel manager before himself examining the corpse.

Suddenly there was a surge as the crowd tried to get close when the inspector reached to remove the stocking mask. Not a sound could be heard as the inspector slowly unpeeled the stocking mask until the face was revealed.

"My Lord, it's Marc!"

"It's Rollande!"

"Look! He's Marc!"

The simultaneous exclamations came from Julian, Taylor, and Belden, as they shouted out in astonishment.

Inspector Parjacques, who had heard them, was quickly there, confronting them, asking questions.

One after another they answered him, identifying Marc Rollande, explaining that he was a member of their vacationing group, all of them repeating over and over again that they couldn't believe he was the cat burglar, despite the evidence there before their eyes.

The police moved efficiently, checking out the hotel room from which Rollande had fallen—it turned out to be the room that Rollande and Genevieve had occupied—and had found nothing there to give them a hint of what had happened. After that they took the body away and cleared out the hotel casino so they could use the place to conduct their investigation. It appeared Rollande had been pushed from the window.

Naturally, since Marc Rollande had been in Monte Carlo with Julian and the others in the group, they all came in for the most intensive questioning by Parjacques. The inspector soon had the full story of all the events that had taken place at Greenlawn in Maryland, as well as in the Bahamas. He learned as well about Pierre Dupin and his two bodyguards—those three had quickly checked out of the hotel after it was discovered that the dead man was Rollande—and about the possible affair that had developed between Genevieve and Belden Robins. So he bore down particularly hard when questioning the latter two separately.

Genevieve readily admitted to the inspector that she and Belden were deeply attracted to one another and that, yes, her husband, Marc, had known of this. But she didn't know, still couldn't believe, that Marc was the cat burglar, nor did she know who could have pushed him out of the window of their room if, as it appeared, someone actually had done that.

Parjacques reached into his coat pocket and held up his hand. "Do you recognize these, Madame?" he asked.

Genevieve looked carefully at the objects in his hand

and nodded. "Yes," she whispered. "Those are my necklaces, rings, and brooch."

"When we searched your husband's body," the inspector said, "these were in his pants pocket."

Genevieve still couldn't understand how Marc could be the cat burglar, nor why he would have gone to all the trouble of dressing up the way he was dressed just to steal her jewels.

When the inspector suggested ever so softly that perhaps she wouldn't be too sorry now to see her husband out of the way, Genevieve replied indignantly that even if *that* were true, she'd had nothing to do with his death, and that certainly she hadn't pushed him from the window; she had witnesses who were with her in the courtyard at the time her husband had plunged from the window.

Parjacques nodded sagely; he had already verified that fact.

Belden Robins, when his turn came to be questioned by the inspector, was equally frank about his feelings for Genevieve. He, too, said that, yes, he knew Rollande was aware of his involvement with Genevieve. He admitted he sometimes worried that Rollande might harm Genevieve. "But if and when the time came, I expected Genevieve to divorce him and marry me," Belden added, shrugging.

The inspector pressed on, saying, nevertheless, surely Monsieur Robins wouldn't be too sorry now to see the husband out of the way. Belden replied much as Genevieve had done at the same suggestion, that even if that were true, he'd had nothing to do with Rollande's death, that he had been in the courtyard at the time it had happened and that there were witnesses who could place him there.

Once more Parjacques nodded sagely; again, as in the case of Genevieve, he had verified that fact.

The following day the police, who had sent out a wanted-for-questioning bulletin on Pierre Dupin and his two companions, had the three men in custody. They had been apprehended at the border, driving a rented Citroën, and escorted back to Monte Carlo for questioning.

All three denied any knowledge of the circumstances of the death of Marc Rollande. All Dupin would tell the inspector was that he and Rollande had been involved in a business deal in the Bahamas and had met several times for discussions in Monte Carlo. Dupin said he had no idea that Rollande was the infamous cat burglar. Dupin was also able to produce witnesses to say that he, Dupin, had been at the gambling tables in the casino at the moment of Rollande's fall from the hotel window.

The other two men, both German, Herr Hesseldorf and Herr Gruner, also claimed they were in and out of the casino the evening of Rollande's death but there were no witnesses—other than Pierre Dupin—who could place them there at the exact time of Rollande's fall. Even though it turned out that Hesseldorf and Gruner had arrest records for assault and extortion in Germany, Inspector Parjacques had no grounds for holding them in the present case.

Perhaps the greatest shock of all to Genevieve and Julian and the others who were with them was that Marc Rollande could have been the cat burglar all Monte Carlo had been talking about for days. It just seemed so difficult to accept even in the face of all the evidence. Certainly they had all been aware that Marc was desperate for money and that the first appearance of the cat burglar coincided with Rollande's arrival in Monte Carlo, but the most striking proof of all was that they had seen it with their own eyes: Marc Rollande dressed in the very clothes the cat burglar had been described as wearing, and with Genevieve's jewels.

The police, for their part, were gratified that they could write finis to the whole business of the jewel thefts. They were happy to see the whole group of Robinses and assorted others depart from Monte Carlo and only too eager to have them take the body of the cat burglar with them.

As for the final burial arrangements for Marc Rollande, Genevieve had decided the most appropriate gesture would be for her to take the body back to France and deliver it to Rollande's relatives for burial. The rest of the group planned to return to America. Genevieve would join them later.

On the morning of the day they were all to depart from Monte Carlo, there was a final ironic twist to the preceding events. In the early morning hours of that day, two policemen spotted a man climbing out of a second-story window of a hotel not far down the road from where the Robinses and their friends had been staying.

The two policemen called out to the man to halt, and when he ignored the order, drew a gun, and fired at them, they returned the fire and shot and killed him on the spot. When they ran to the dead man and saw him clearly they were astounded. He was dressed in a black turtleneck sweater, black slacks, black knitted cap, and black canvas shoes, and was wearing a stocking mask—the outfit of the cat burglar.

When other police reached the scene and made a search of the body, they found that the dead man was carrying several delicate scarves faintly perfumed with the scent found on the scarves used by the cat burglar to gag his victims—items that had not been found on the body of Marc Rollande. This man, too, had stolen jewels and other valuables in his possession.

Within the next few hours, the police were able to determine the man's identity through a check of his fingerprints. He turned out to be an Englishman named William St. Clair, who had a long record of arrests for jewel robberies in England, France, and Belgium. When the police located the quarters where he was staying in Monte Carlo, they uncovered there a cache of jewels stolen in all the known cases of thefts by the cat burglar up until the time Marc Rollande fell from the window of his hotel room. There seemed little doubt but that this man, William St. Clair, was the authentic cat burglar who had created such a furor in Monte Carlo in recent days. Even the scented scarves were in the room.

For a long time afterward Inspector Parjacques pondered the puzzle of Marc Rollande's death, and of why Rollande had been dressed in the disguise of the cat burglar. If—as seemed the most likely possibility—Rollande wanted to steal his wife's jewelry and make her think the robbery was the work of the cat burglar, that would explain why he was dressed in the disguise. It would also explain why he had sent for her to come to their room—so she would see what she thought was the cat burglar escaping out the window.

But it did not explain who was responsible for Rollande's death. That has remained a conundrum to the police and to those who knew Marc Rollande until this day.

Soon after Julian and Janice returned from Monte Carlo, they were in Manhattan when a robbery occurred at their Greenlawn estate where Dorina was staying alone. That poor woman told police a terrifying story of how she awakened in the middle of the night to find three masked men in her darkened room. They had swiftly overpowered and bound and gagged and blindfolded her.

She was left like that all night. It wasn't until the gardener arrived the next morning, found the front door standing open and no one about, and investigated, that she was found and freed. Dorina, though badly shaken, immediately phoned the police.

Once the police were at the house, they discovered an unfathomable fact: Although there were many valuables everywhere in the house, the robbers had confined their search to the servants' quarters which they turned upside down. Dorina, after making a survey of the rooms, could find nothing missing. Nor could she provide the police with any real description of the three housebreakers; events had occurred too swiftly and it had been dark in the room.

When Julian and Janice hurried back to Greenlawn at the report of the robbery, they were unable to find anything missing from the house either. The incident remained inexplicable.

CHAPTER 4

SLEIGHT OF HAND

COPY OF AN UNSIGNED LETTER RECEIVED BY CAPTAIN GREGORY WALTHAM, MARYLAND STATE POLICE, MAILED FROM NEW YORK CITY:

Dear Captain Waltham:

Because I know it will be of personal interest to you, I am writing to tell you that a recent death, which you and everyone else thought was accidental, was in fact murder. I know. I was there at the time and I alone have ferreted out the truth of what happened.

As you may already have surmised, I am referring to the untimely demise of Belden Robins in the south of France. You know that at the time of his death in the swimming pool at the summer home of his recent bride, in the countryside of southern France, the official police verdict was that he had drowned accidentally while swimming alone.

To arrive at the truth, I shall first have to tell you all the pertinent facts preceding his death as I know them.

These facts begin in late July of this year, directly after Belden Robins and his new bride, Genevieve Robins Rollande Robins (to list her correctly by her various married names), returned from a honeymoon cruise around the world. It was then that Belden and Genevieve decided to have a house party at her country place and to invite all of Belden's family—the Robins family—and all those who were connected to Genevieve at Robins Cosmetics.

So, present at the time were Genevieve, Belden, all the Robinses—Taylor, Rebecca, Jonathan, Laura, Benjamin, Daphne, and Dorothy—and Julian and Janice Shields and Pamela and David MacGuffin. Julian and Janice had brought along Dorina Wales, as well. After her horrible experience at the Greenlawn estate in Maryland the last time Julian and Janice were absent, that poor woman was frightened to death to stay there while they were away. They hired an armed security service to protect the house (not that that is germane to this story).

In addition to the names I have just enumerated (and you will have deduced that the name of the writer of this letter is among them), there were others who put in appearances from time to time, as we shall see.

The summer house was a gracious and pleasant retreat, large, airy, quaintly old-fashioned yet equipped with all the modern conveniences, as were the grounds.

There were tennis courts, stables with six riding horses, an outdoor swimming pool with a newly installed hot tub on the terrace, as well as a putting green.

The women in the group went horseback riding more than the men, the younger men spent more time playing tennis, and the older men were, more often than not, on the putting green. Following these activities, most everyone, at different times, would take advantage of the hot tub and then go for a swim in the pool.

Belden and Genevieve had hired a middle-aged French couple, Marie and André Sebastian, she as cook, he to serve the meals, and the dinners each night were a high point of the holiday. Dorina, who was so accustomed to the role of housekeeper, could not refrain from making suggestions to the Sebastians the day she arrived. Fortunately for all, her suggestions were tolerated with good grace by the French couple.

One evening Belden and Genevieve had a string quartet from the closest village come in and play for the guests.

On another evening, for fun, they hired an old woman who was renowned locally for forecasting the future to entertain the guests by telling their fortunes from a reading of the palms of their hands.

The woman, Lucia Comte, was white-haired, wrinkled, and thin as a scarecrow, and few of the guests, men or women, could suppress a small shiver of nervous anticipation when she turned one of their palms upward. Her own hands were gnarled and bony as a skeleton's.

Of course, everyone there was sophisticated enough to know that this ritual was only harmless make-believe, a feeling that was reinforced as she went from palm to palm, reciting a litany of long life, many riches, and happiness for each one.

But when she reached Genevieve's palm, she dropped the new bride's hand as if it were a hot poker, muttering that she saw so much death there, so much death of others near to Genevieve.

Well, at that point, some of the playfulness of the game went out of the evening. (Later, of course, all the guests realized that the two past tragedies Genevieve had suffered, the deaths of her former husbands, James and Marc, were probably common gossip in the area and that the old woman would have heard it.)

At the moment, however, all present were admittedly unsettled. A situation that only grew worse when Lucia Comte peered next into Belden's palm, gave a grieving cry, and stood, backing away from him, shaking her head and whispering, "No more, no more."

She departed as quickly as possible, leaving a pall of gloom behind. Poor Belden manfully tried to shrug off the whole business as pure nonsense. Soon after, everyone retired for the night.

But early the next morning when the whole household was awakened by a veritable cacophony of alarms, it was not to find that Belden Robins had suffered a terrible fate but that that poor unfortunate, Dorina Wales, had. She was found in her room, once again bound, gagged, and blindfolded as she had been at Greenlawn, only this time she was dead, having silently choked to death on the gag thrust into her mouth. Once again, too, her room had been thoroughly ransacked. The poor creature had not been able to escape her Appointment in Samarra, after all.

The local police, when they arrived in due course, spent very little time at the house. They gave it as their opinion that Dorina's murder had been the result of a simple robbery gone wrong. For several months now, the local police had been plagued by one robbery after another. Nor was Dorina the first one to die during the course of these robberies. Twice before the victims had choked to death on the gags thrust into their mouths. The police believed that the robberies were the work of a gang of thugs who had appeared recently in the area. The robbery and death of Dorina were just one more piece of the thugs' handiwork.

Although this letter is being written to you about the later death/murder of Belden Robins, there are two matters relating to Dorina that should be noted here, even though they may have no significance.

One occurred on the morning of her arrival here at the house, a day later than all the guests had arrived. She had stayed overnight in Paris to do some shopping for Janice. Since there was no other way for her to reach the house except by car, Belden and Genevieve had had André Sebastian drive in to pick her and her luggage up. David MacGuffin, who said he wanted to get a few items in the city, went along.

The first of the two matters I mentioned occurred when the three of them returned to the house and began to carry in the luggage. Dorina set up a great hue and cry that one of her suitcases was missing. She was absolutely distraught that the suitcase wasn't there. She was sure she had had André Sebastian put it in the car, along with all the other packages and luggage and now it was gone. The oddest thing was that, when she was asked by those at the house if that particular suitcase had contained any valuable property, she kept shaking her head and saying no, no, no.

MacGuffin had helped André carry the luggage into the house after Dorina had been detained outside, and both men said they did not take a suitcase such as she described to the bedroom assigned to her in the house. André said he vaguely remembered placing such a suitcase in the car in Paris, but he couldn't be sure. In any event, whether or not that was the suitcase in question, it had now disappeared. Dorina continued to despair over losing it and finally, as an explanation, said it had sentimental value to her because it had belonged to her late husband, Alfred.

The second of the matters relating to Dorina concerned the bedroom she was given at the house. Up until the very morning she arrived, André Sebastian and his wife, Marie, had occupied that room and had switched, with the approval of Genevieve, only a short time before Dorina reached the house. If, as the police reasoned, the robbery and subsequent murder of Dorina had been a random burglary by a gang of thugs, it was sheer fate that had placed Dorina in the room to die instead of the Sebastians.

The above account disposes of the events surrounding Dorina and now I want to get to the real point of my letter which, as circumstances would have it, took place the morning following the murder of Dorina.

Stated bluntly, early on that morning, Belden Robins

was found drowned in the swimming pool. According to Genevieve, Belden had arisen very early, saying he was going to take a swim in the pool before the others were up, and telling Genevieve to go back to sleep, which she did.

More than an hour passed before Genevieve arose and went downstairs herself. The others were also just arising and coming down for breakfast. There was no sign of Belden. Genevieve sent André to look for him, thinking perhaps he was somewhere on the grounds or in the stables. André was the one who discovered Belden at the bottom of the swimming pool, dove in, pulled him out, and shouted for help. Everyone in the house rushed out. Belden was beyond help and had been for some time.

The police had to be called again. This time after they arrived, they sent for an inspector from Paris to conduct an investigation.

Inspector Charles Arouet (as you are aware, I know, since you have been in correspondence with him) made up his mind from the beginning that Belden's death was an accidental drowning, and I don't think he ever considered any other possibility.

This belief was based upon the following considerations: There were no signs or marks of violence upon the body, and Belden was a young, physically fit, powerful man who would have fought fiercely against anyone who tried to drown him in the pool; moreover, a thorough autopsy of the body revealed no suspicious causes for death other than drowning. There the verdict has rested.

Inspector Arouet, who strikes me as somewhat of a romantic, suggested that perhaps what led to the accidental drowning was—as the inspector so poetically put it—"the ardors of the new bridegroom still on his honeymoon."

One possibility that was never considered and that could easily explain how Belden might have been overcome and deliberately murdered by drowning lies in another direction. I am referring to the hot tub. If he had been in there, not in the pool, relaxed up to his chin in soothing water, how very easy it would have been for anyone, anyone at all, to sneak up, lean down, push his head under water, and hold it there until he was dead.

An accidental drowning, indeed.

Belden Robins was deliberately drowned in the hot tub. Then his body was placed in the swimming pool.

I offer this correct theory to you to pursue and to apprehend the guilty party.

Sincerely yours,
ONE WHO SEEKS JUSTICE

CHAPTER 5

THE MISSING HEIR

ONE OF THE MOST ASTONISHING TURNS of events in a series of astonishing events—in the case known as The Revenge of the Robins Family—was the sudden appearance of a young man professing to be the illegitimate son of the dead Tyler Robins. Proof of that fact would make him a claimant to the Robins fortune.

The young man in question, who said his name was Charles Atherton Robins, presented himself one day at the Paris office of Robins Cosmetics and asked to see Julian Shields.

After the unhappy holidays Julian and the others had spent at Genevieve's summer house in the south of France, they had all returned to Paris for a brief stay and to look into the affairs of Robins Cosmetics' French operation before returning home. Thus it was that Julian was at the company's Paris office that day.

As soon as the young man was ushered into Julian's office and announced his name and said who his father had been, Julian was struck by the uncanny resemblance this young man bore to one of Tyler's dead sons, James. It was as if James were standing there in the office, except for one difference: Charles Atherton Robins, as he called himself, spoke with a pronounced British accent.

"Well, well," was all Julian could manage at the moment.

"I quite appreciate that my turning up like this is bound to be as much of a shock to you, and others, as it is for me to have just discovered who my father was," Charles Robins said. "I think you'll understand better when I tell you my story."

Julian, flustered as he was, made the young man comfortable and sat back to listen to his story.

Charles Atherton Robins, according to the tale he now told, had been born twenty-seven years earlier in Switzerland. His mother had been British, Lady Jean Atherton, daughter of Lord Robert Atherton, a wealthy English importer of tea and herbs.

The young man, Charles, had believed from birth that his own father was dead, a story he had been told by his mother and his grandfather, who wished to keep the truth of his birth secret from him. What he had been told was that his father was a Swiss businessman—the Robins last name had been recorded on his birth certificate but the first name of the father had been changed to

Theodore—who had died in a motorcar accident a month before Charles was born.

Charles had never questioned these facts, indeed, never had had reason to question them, as he was growing up in England. Nor did anyone else who knew him, his mother, or her family. There had always been plenty of money and, after graduating from Cambridge, Charles had become a solicitor. His grandfather's once-thriving business had long since gone bankrupt after the death of the old man while Charles had been still in school.

For some years past, Charles said, his mother had been bedridden with a chronic heart disease and had died just a fortnight ago. Before she died, she had told him the true story of his parentage: that his real father had been the rich American businessman Tyler Robins.

Almost thirty years earlier Lady Jean Atherton had met and fallen madly in love. Tyler Robins was already married at the time and they saw one another on the trips Tyler made alone to England. When Lady Jean found she was going to have Tyler's child, she, her father, and Tyler agreed upon a plan in order to avoid the scandal should the true circumstances ever be revealed.

The plan, which was carried out, was that Lady Jean should go on a holiday to Switzerland. While there, she wrote back to all her friends—and Lord Atherton told the same story around—that she had met a Swiss businessman, Theodore Robins, and they had married. Later, she wrote that her husband had been killed in an automobile accident and she was expecting a child. After the birth of Charles, she and the baby had returned to London.

"All these past years," Charles said, "I would read

about the wealthy American Robins family and never once did I realize they were related to me. It simply never entered my head that my father could have been anyone other than a Swiss businessman who was dead. When mother told me who my real father was, she said she had waited until anyone who could have been hurt by the truth was dead. But she felt I should be entitled to claim my legal inheritance."

He had with him, Charles said, his birth certificate and dozens of photographs of Tyler, his mother, and himself together taken when he was a baby. His mother had given them to him at the time she told him the story. He now produced them and spread them across the desk where Julian was sitting.

Julian was virtually speechless as he studied the photographs. Even at that early age, the baby in the photographs was clearly the young man sitting across the desk, the woman was a very beautiful brunette, and the man—the man was Tyler, looking handsome, vigorous, and rakish. There were snapshots of one or another of the adults holding the baby, of the couple kissing and hugging. What's more, Julian decided, the photographs looked to be not doctored but authentic. Although he would, in time, certainly document that fact.

"I knew you were now running Robins Cosmetics," Charles said. "Once I had settled affairs after my mother's funeral was over, I tried to contact you at your New York City office. When they told me you were here in Paris, I came over yesterday and, well, here I am."

"Yes," Julian answered slowly, "I guess I should say welcome." He added, "There are others here in Paris right now who will, I'm sure, be anxious to see you."

Julian then suggested that they meet that evening at Genevieve's Paris apartment, and he gave Charles the address, saying, as he pointed to the photographs and the birth certificate, "Please bring these with you."

After Charles Robins left, Julian spent the remainder of the day discussing this unexpected development with Genevieve, Pamela and David MacGuffin, and Janice. The Taylor Robins family was also in Paris, having returned there from Genevieve's summer place, and it was agreed that they, too, should be present at Genevieve's apartment that evening to listen to the young man's story.

By a few minutes to 8 P.M.—the time set by Julian for Charles Robins to arrive—all the others were there and had been told by Julian the story Charles Robins had related to him.

"I think the man's an out-and-out impostor," David MacGuffin kept saying over and over again.

Taylor Robins, on the other hand, suggested that they wait and see for themselves. "The story could just be true. We all know and can say it aloud now that when Tyler was still alive, he was always a great one for the ladies."

Soon after, Charles Atherton Robins was there, being introduced around by Julian.

Genevieve had her maid serve drinks and Charles Robins repeated the story he had told Julian and produced his birth certificate and the photographs.

Julian, watching for a reaction from those meeting Charles Robins for the first time, could tell they were impressed with him and with the pictures. The newcomer, if he was who he said he was, was clearly a charming person. They were all drawn to him, mostly because he was so much a replica of the dead James. Genevieve, even more than the others, was clearly enchanted with him, which was understandable since she had been so much in love with James when they were married.

At the conclusion of the evening, Charles Robins expressed his delight at meeting all of them and said, "Look here now, you have been most kind to me, a stranger to you until today. I realize that you would like to affirm for yourselves the truth of what I've told you. Therefore, I would like to leave with you these photographs and a copy, which I have had made, of my birth certificate. I shall wait to hear from you." He gave them the name and the telephone number of the hotel where he was staying in Paris, and departed.

"How extraordinary!" Rebecca Robins exclaimed when he'd left. "One feels he's genuine."

When MacGuffin still expressed some reservations about whether or not he was an impostor, Taylor cut him off. "Naturally, every effort should be made to determine the truth of what he's told us. Once that's done, however, and if it's proved true, then I shall forget any claims I think I may have against Tyler's estate and I will destroy the second will in favor of this young man's receiving his rightful share and taking his place in the family and in Robins Cosmetics. I believe my dead brother would wish this."

The others in the room seemed to agree. Julian, especially, was impressed with Taylor's words. It appeared, Julian thought, that all Taylor had wanted all along was to have a Robins family member in the cosmetics company. Well, he, Julian, could live with that.

During the course of the next several days, Julian used all the resources at his command to establish the authenticity of the photographs and the birth certificate. At the end of that time, the photographs, after being examined by several experts at detecting forgeries, were declared to be originals. A birth certificate was on file in Berne, Switzerland, for a Charles Atherton Robins, born twenty-seven years before. The mother's maiden name was listed as Jean Atherton, the father as Theodore Robins. From London, Julian received confirmation that the Charles Robins now in Paris was, as he had said, the son of the now-deceased Jean Atherton Robins and the grandson of the late Lord Robert Atherton.

With this information in hand, Charles Robins was welcomed into the Robins family and, in time, arrangements would be made for him to have a financial share of the estate as well as to join Robins Cosmetics' board of directors.

"I for one am delighted at the turn of events," Taylor Robins said at a party given at Genevieve's apartment to celebrate the occasion—a remark that drew applause from the others.

It was clear to all present that Genevieve was equally delighted. During the past several days she and Charles had been virtually inseparable and that very evening announced that they planned to marry, certain as they were that they were in love with one another, despite the short time they'd been together. This announcement, too, brought applause. They set the wedding date for the end of the same week because they all had to return to America by the weekend, Charles now going with them. Genevieve wanted to be married in Paris and to have a simple wedding in her apartment.

The women immediately set about planning the wedding and a wedding announcement and photograph of Genevieve were sent to newspapers in Paris, London, and New York.

This last action produced two unexpected and unfortunate results.

One was the appearance of a young lady from England. She had read the news in the London papers and said that she was Charles Robins's fiancee. Her name was Penny Lattimore.

The other unfortunate result was that poor Genevieve began receiving anonymous threatening letters and phone calls. All appeared to originate with the same person and all gave dire warning that there would be fatal consequences suffered by Genevieve and her husband-to-be unless the wedding was canceled. All the communications were in French, the verbal ones in a guttural tone of voice.

Charles Robins made light of the claims by Penny Lattimore on his affections.

"We were never engaged," he explained to Genevieve and the others who had gathered at Genevieve's apartment while Penny was there protesting that Charles was supposed to marry her.

"Look, love," Charles said to her in front of the others, "you know we were never that serious about one another."

"I was!" Penny wailed.

Charles patiently explained to everyone listening that he and Penny had simply dated, had a lot of laughs together, and the whole affair had been simply one of fun. Certainly, he said, at no time had he ever expressed any serious intentions toward Penny.

Everyone there was inclined to believe his words. It was clear that Penny, while a pretty little thing, blond and green-eyed, was probably simply creating a dramatic scene.

Nevertheless, the situation might have continued somewhat sticky had it not been that Benjamin Robins was immediately attracted to Penny and made his feelings evident. So she was mollified and in turn took to him, especially after Benjamin suggested that she stay over in Paris and let him show her the city, and remain for the wedding.

One evening during this time Julian took the whole group on a tour of the Robins Cosmetics plant and laboratories on the outskirts of Paris. The workers and chemists had all gone home for the day, and Julian was able to show them how the various products were chemically created. All of them were delighted with this behind-the-scenes look, especially Penny Lattimore.

But the matter of the threatening phone calls and letters was not to be so lightly dismissed, and grew uglier as the day for the wedding came closer.

Julian and Genevieve, especially, speculated that the source of the threats was someone who had been connected to Genevieve's recent husband Marc Rollande. A friend, perhaps, or a member of Rollande's family, who suspected that she might have played a part in his murder.

With the ominous threat hanging in the air, the wedding, when it finally took place, was a tense affair. Special security guards had been hired to keep out all intruders that day. And it wasn't until Genevieve and Charles were officially declared man and wife, without an incident to mar the ceremony, that everyone was able to draw a vast sigh of relief.

There was one minor puzzling absence from the wedding: Julian Shields was not present. He had phoned Janice about an hour before the ceremony was to begin and asked her to inform Genevieve and Charles that he had been unavoidably detained but would see them the following day when they would all fly to America together.

The reason for Julian's absence did not become clear until that evening when he asked all the others, except for Genevieve and Charles, who were honeymooning at her apartment, to join him for dinner at the hotel where he and Janice were staying.

It was then that he dropped his bombshell: That afternoon, even as the wedding was taking place, he had been making further inquiries about Charles Atherton Robins, inquiries that had proved beyond any doubt that the story Charles had told about being Tyler's son was untrue. There was no doubt about it, Julian stated firmly: The young man was an impostor!

An immediate hubbub of protests broke out from all those who had believed so completely the young man's story, especially Taylor Robins.

Julian quieted them by carefully explaining: "With all the checking we did on his background, it suddenly occurred to me—and I don't know where the thought came from—that there was one area we had completely overlooked. That area was the precise whereabouts of Tyler Robins at the time he was alleged to have been involved with Lady Jean Atherton some twenty-seven to thirty years ago."

He paused to let them absorb that thought before he continued: "Actually, it wasn't so difficult to come by the information. All it took was a couple of transatlantic phone calls to the New York office. And the fact is that Tyler Robins did not make his first trip to England until twenty-five years ago. He could not have been involved with Jean Atherton. Charles cannot be his son!"

There was stunned silence in the room when Julian had concluded his remarks.

Taylor was the one who finally spoke: "'And I was so sure he was telling the truth."

"Yes, you were, dear," Rebecca, Taylor's wife, answered sympathetically.

A group discussion followed, with all those involved agreeing that there was no point in informing Genevieve or Charles of this shocking piece of information, now that the marriage had taken place. And that Julian should speak to Charles first after they had all returned to America.

The following day they were all together again at Charles de Gaulle Airport, Julian and Janice, Genevieve and Charles, Pamela and David MacGuffin, and the Taylor Robins family: Taylor, Rebecca, Jonathan, Laura, Daphne, Dorothy, and Benjamin. And Benjamin had talked Penny Lattimore into going with them for a holiday in the United States. They were flying out of Charles de Gaulle Airport, on Air France's Concorde.

Both Julian and Janice had flown on the Concorde before but to the other twelve it was an exciting first experience to fly at a speed of 1,300 miles per hour at a height of between 50,000 and 60,000 feet.

The group occupied fourteen of the forty seats in the forward section of the plane's two cabins, sitting two by two with much changing about of seats as the flight progressed out over the Atlantic. This shifting about of seating arrangements was, somewhat later, to become of crucial interest in view of the murder that was to transpire on board before the Concorde touched down in the United States.

For a time, early in the flight, Julian and Janice sat side by side in the first two seats with, behind them, Pamela and David side by side; then Taylor and Rebecca Robins, Charles and Genevieve, Benjamin and Penny Lattimore, with Jonathan sitting beside his sister, Dorothy, while the other two Robins daughters, Laura and Daphne, sat together. At various times after that the twosomes rearranged themselves.

The period of time that was to become of critical importance was rather late in the flight, just after they had all been served champagne.

Taylor Robins had left his seat at that point to have a word with Genevieve, taking his filled champagne glass with him. Charles had moved from his seat beside Genevieve to talk to David MacGuffin whose mystery novels Charles had read. Charles left his champagne-filled glass behind on a table at his seat. Pamela had moved to stand in the aisle and talk to Julian and Janice. Pamela then returned to her own seat.

When Taylor returned to his seat, his wife, Rebecca,

left briefly to talk to her children Laura and Daphne and then returned to find Julian and Taylor talking together, Julian standing in the aisle. Penny had, meanwhile, gone to sit beside Genevieve. Janice briefly joined Julian in the aisle at the seats where Taylor and Rebecca sat.

Soon after that, Charles returned to his seat, Penny returned to hers, and Julian and Janice went back to their original seats, as another round of champagne was being served.

Moments later, Taylor, talking to Rebecca, paused, took a deep drink of his champagne, and almost instantaneously grabbed his throat; his eyes glazed over, the glass fell from his hands, and his body tumbled off the seat and fell, sprawled, into the aisle.

Rebecca screamed and screamed and almost immediately the aisle around where Taylor's body lay was filled with people, one of the stewardesses pushing through and ordering them back until the plane's captain arrived. The captain felt for Taylor's pulse, could find none, and softly announced that Taylor was dead.

The captain would testify later that the dead man's skin had turned a violent pink and that he, the captain, was struck by the powerful odor of almonds emanating from the body, which he had once read indicated the presence of ingested cyanide. He suspected, he said, this was a case of poisoning, farfetched as it might have seemed only minutes earlier. He confiscated the empty champagne glass lying near the body and had the glass carefully wrapped in cellophane which the stewardess brought him. The next step the captain took was to have the body wrapped in a blanket and removed to the cockpit. From there news of the death was radioed ahead to

Dulles International Airport in Virginia where the Concorde was due shortly.

In time, during the autopsy and subsequent inquest into the death of Taylor Robins, large and small facts became a part of the official record.

Death was caused by cyanide poisoning.

Cyanide was found in the champagne glass from which Taylor had drunk.

At the moment he died, the Concorde was at longitude 78, latitude 24, an ironic touch.

Witnesses who had observed Taylor in the brief time between the serving of the champagne and his drinking the fatal draft testified that to the best of their knowledge he had not tasted the contents of his glass up until that final moment. Rebecca, Julian, Janice, Charles and Genevieve—who were sitting directly behind Taylor and Rebecca—and the stewardess all stated that to the best of their recollection his glass was still full when the second round of champagne was served.

No one could say that Taylor's glass had been switched with someone else's before he drank from it.

As to where the cyanide might have come from, Julian established the fact that there had been cyanide present in the Robins Cosmetics laboratories on the outskirts of Paris which the group had visited before they had taken the flight. The cyanide there was sometimes used in new-products experiments, Julian explained.

He also testified that any one of those visiting the laboratories during that tour could have surreptitiously stolen a small quantity of the cyanide—without being observed. "Who could have considered such a possibility?" he concluded sadly.

The strongest suspicion in the murder was directed toward Charles Atherton Robins because of his recent, and curious, relationship with the family, especially the now-proven falsity of the story of his background as he had related it. Julian had had to reveal these facts to the authorities.

Charles had seemed to be genuinely bewildered when Julian finally had to tell him he was an impostor. Genevieve still stood loyally behind her new husband. The police, lacking any other evidence to link Charles with the cyanide poisoning, could not detain him.

There the matter of the murder of Taylor Robins rested.

A few days later, Taylor Robins's body was cremated, according to his wishes, and the ashes buried in a cemetery in Illinois, next to the grave of his son, Belden, who had died in France.

All the remaining members of the family were there for the services: Rebecca, Benjamin, Jonathan, Laura, Dorothy, and Daphne, as well as Julian and Janice, Genevieve and Charles, Pamela and David, and Penny Lattimore. Paul Bryce also flew up from New Jersey.

It was plain to everyone there that Taylor Robins's two sons, Benjamin and Jonathan, could barely conceal their hostility to Julian Shields and Charles Robins, the inference being that Benjamin and Jonathan suspected that one or the other, Julian or Charles, was responsible for Taylor's murder.

CHAPTER 6

VOICES FROM THE GRAVE

COPY OF A TAPE RECORDING MADE BY DAVID MACGUFFIN FOLLOWING THE DEATHS OF DORINA WALES AND BELDEN ROBINS, RECEIVED BY MACGUFFIN IN NEW YORK AFTER HE MAILED IT TO HIMSELF FROM FRANCE:

I am recording this message (in case something happens to me) concerning two recent deaths, or perhaps more, to which I may accidentally have discovered the key, or one of the keys. A couple of days ago Dorina Wales, the housekeeper for Julian and Janice, arrived here at Genevieve's summer house. I drove into Paris with André Sebastian to pick up Dorina and bring her out to the house. It strikes me now that she appeared somewhat agitated even when we first met her in Paris. She had been shopping for Genevieve and she had a load of packages and baggage. I helped André put them into the trunk of the car. Dorina appeared reluctant to give up the last bag, a worn suitcase, but since there was no room for it inside the car, she gave it to me. She and André had already gotten into the car. As I placed the suitcase into the car trunk, the snaps on the suitcase flew open enough for me to see that the only thing inside was another bag, this one a cowhide attaché case, which struck me as extremely odd! As I glanced at the attaché case, what struck me as even more odd was that I had seen the same attaché case before, or an attaché case so similar as to be identical. George Pittman had brought it with him to the Bahamas. I remembered I had seen him with it there and in his cottage before he was killed. I do not remember seeing it in the cottage after he was killed, nor do I remember noting that it was missing after he was killed. I would probably never have thought of the attaché case again if I hadn't seen it in the suitcase Dorina handed to me. I snapped the suitcase shut but thought to myself, I'm determined to see what's inside that bag or my name isn't MacGuffin. As soon as we got to Genevieve's house, I made sure I took out the battered suitcase, along with some other packages, and hurried inside, ahead of Dorina who was distracted by Julian and Janice greeting her at the car. On the way to the room I was told Dorina would occupy, I stopped off in my own room and hid the suitcase away in a closet there, then took the other packages to Dorina's room. Shortly afterward Dorina created a big scene and fuss about her missing suitcase. My plan then was simply to take a look at the contents of the attaché case and return it and the suitcase to her.

Unfortunately, I had no opportunity to examine the attaché case that evening since every time I was in my room, Pamela was there as well and I did not want to involve her in this business—at least until I had a chance to find out what it was all about. That chance did not come until the following day, yesterday, and what a day it was! We all were awakened to find that Dorina had been killed during the night—the police said by a gang of thugs from the area—and the police were trampling all over the place. Knowing that Dorina's suitcase was hidden in my closet, I was terrified that they might make a search of the house, find the suitcase (I still didn't know what it contained), and arrest me for her murder. One of the curses of being a mystery writer is having too much imagination at times, and this was one of them. But since the police decided her death had been the result of an outside robbery, they had no interest in the rest of us. So it wasn't until late in the afternoon that I was able finally to go to my bedroom, lock the door, and take out the attaché case. I immediately saw that I was right about its belonging to George Pittman. His G.P. initials were stamped on it. I opened the case and saw that inside was a leather-bound book and a short reel of recording tape. It wasn't until I opened the book and read on the first page the words PROPERTY OF EVELYN ROBINS *that I realized I held in my hands the much-discussed lost diary, which of course it was. I read through it eagerly, needless to say, seeking a clue or clues to—to, well, whatever. When I finished reading it page by page, I must confess I was disappointed. It was mostly an account of her daily observations about her husband and children and a few others in her life, her concerns and the provisions she had made for those around her after her husband's death. She had planned to marry Julian Shields and before her own death had made sure he would run the Robins Cosmetics company. And she had seen to it that her grandchildren were also provided for since their fathers were dead: the child—unborn at that time—of Genevieve; Marsha, Pamela's daughter; Molly and her mother, Carrie—as well as a Dr. John Forbes. Forbes had died around the same time as Evelyn herself, but she hadn't known that in time to change her provisions. The only real shocker in the diary was that Tyler Robins did suspect that Evelyn was having an affair with another man, this Dr. John Forbes. That's there in the diary! So the diary would help prove Taylor Robins's claim that Tyler had suspected Evelyn, had cut her out of his own will, and had substituted Taylor instead. But otherwise, as I said, there wasn't much I could see in the diary that would raise eyebrows. I then turned to the reel of recording tape and played it back on my machine. It was very brief, a conversation beween Tyler Robins and Paul Bryce, which I shall now quote. Tyler speaks first, saying, quote, Paul, I have a—ah—rather delicate matter I want to discuss with you. End quote. Bryce, quote, Go ahead, let's hear it. End quote. Tyler, quote, It concerns dealings you have had with Ernest Truax. End quote. Bryce, quote, Who? I don't know what— End quote. Tyler, quote, Ernest Truax, my employee. Come on, Paul, let's not play games. I have documents, photographs, proving you made payoffs to Truax to buy information on new products Robins Cosmetics has developed. I hired an investigator. I have proof of what you've been doing. End quote. Bryce, quote, I don't want to discuss this—End quote. Tyler, quote, There's nothing to discuss. If I took you to court, it would all come out; you'd be ruined. I have another solution. End quote. Bryce, quote, Look, Tyler, I am not going to discuss this— End quote. Tyler, quote, The solution is that you will pay me five million dollars, off the books, and that'll be the end of the matter. You have a choice, one or the other. And you have until the end of the cruise to decide which it'll be. Now, let's have another drink. Pass me your glass. . . . End quote. End of the tape. After I finished listening to the tape, I went back to Evelyn Robins's diary. There had been references there to this tape. I reread those entries. Evelyn had of course known about the recording and, in fact, probably had it with her—along with her diary—when she died in the Greek Isles and both diary and tape disappeared. In the diary, Evelyn mentions that she told Julian Shields—at that time the family's lawyer—about the tape recording between Paul Bryce and her husband. I was curious, too, about the mention Tyler made on the tape to hiring an investigator to get proof on Bryce and Truax. That investigator had to have been B. J. Grieg. In the diary, Evelyn writes that Grieg always handled her husband's investigations. And she, too, had hired Grieg to investigate Tyler's death. So Grieg had known all about Bryce and Truax, and probably had plenty on both of them even though the tape—until now—had been missing. Hmm. Could it have been this tape that everybody was after and the diary only a red herring?*

Another thought: How did this tape and this diary come to be in Dorina's possession? At the time Evelyn Robins died in the Greek Isles, and the tape and diary disappeared, both George Pittman and Alfred Wales were there. Later, both Pittman and Alfred were murdered in the Bahamas where, according to Taylor Robins's testimony at the time, Pittman had said he could produce the diary. Did someone kill first the one and then the other for the diary, and still not find it? At this point, I have no theories. But I do want to add that this morning, before I recorded this message, Belden Robins was found drowned in Genevieve's swimming pool—yet another death. Which is why I am making this tape recording and mailing it back to myself in New York at the earliest possible moment. I do not mean to sound melodramatic but in the event that something should happen to me, I want this information to be known and the existence of the Tyler-Bryce tape recording and Evelyn Robins's diary to be revealed. To further protect them, I shall take a safe-deposit box at the Banc Metropolis in Paris upon my return there and mail the key to myself along with this recording. If nothing happens to me, I shall—in time—turn both over to the proper authorities. This is David MacGuffin speaking from the summer house of Genevieve Robins. . . .

CHAPTER 7

POLICE PROCEDURAL

1. Q. AND A.

Q.: Please state your full name for the record.
A.: Benjamin Cunningham Robins.
Q.: I will read to you now the Miranda waiver which you have signed. The first question on the waiver was: Have you read or had read to you the warnings as to your rights? You answered yes. Is that correct?
A.: That is correct.
Q.: The second question was: Do you under-

stand these rights? You answered yes. Is that correct?

A.: That is correct.

Q.: Third question: Do you wish to answer any questions? You answered yes. Is that correct?

A.: That is correct.

Q.: And you signed this waiver of your own free will?

A.: I did.

Q.: Now, did you know Penelope Lattimore of Eleven-nineteen East Sixth Street, Manhattan?

A.: I did.

Q.: And what was your relationship with Penelope Lattimore?

A.: I—we were good friends.

Q.: You lived together until quite recently, is that correct?

A.: We lived together for three months.

Q.: Until she moved out, two weeks ago? And took her own place, in Greenwich Village?

A.: She—we—decided to live apart for a while.

Q.: Up until then you had thought the two of you were to be married?

A.: We had discussed it, yes.

Q.: And after she moved away, did you still think you were going to be married?

A.: She said she wanted to think about it; that's why we were going to live apart for a while.

Q.: Actually, isn't it more accurate to say that

you still wanted to get married, but she didn't?

A.: You know how women get sometimes, can't make up their minds.

Q.: But that wasn't the case here, was it? According to people we've questioned who knew both of you, she had made up her mind she wasn't going to marry you. And she moved out of your apartment because she was frightened of you?

A.: No, that's not true. She wasn't afraid of me.

Q.: But afraid of what you might do? Didn't she tell people you had an irrational need to avenge your father's death? That you had said you were going to get the two men you thought killed your father?

A.: I don't know what she told people. Or what people have said that she told them.

Q.: Julian Shields and Charles Robins. Those were the two men, weren't they?

A.: I've already told you that I don't know what she told people.

Q.: Now, we come to the afternoon of December eleventh. You went to Penelope Lattimore's apartment that day? There's a witness who saw you arrive at the building.

A.: Mrs. Kurch. I know. She looks like the type, a snoop, always watching everybody who goes in and out down there.

Q.: How do you know her name?

A.: I saw her watching me from her first floor

window when I left. Earlier, in the hallway, I noticed the name on her door after I came downstairs.

Q.: So, you admit you did go to Penelope Lattimore's apartment that day, December eleventh?

A.: Yes, to talk to her. She had phoned me and asked me to come.

Q.: So you've told us. For the record, what time did she phone you?

A.: About three o'clock, an hour or so before I went there.

Q.: We've checked the telephone company's records for all calls made from the telephone in that apartment. Your number was not among them.

A.: Maybe she made the call from outside, from a pay telephone; she didn't say where she was calling from.

Q.: You went to her apartment; you went upstairs. Then what happened?

A.: The door was unlocked. I could see it was standing ajar a couple of inches. I knocked on the door; I called to her. There was no answer.

Q.: What did you do then?

A.: I pushed the door back and went in and—

Q.: Hold it a minute! You pushed the door open, how?

A.: With my hand.

Q.: How with your hand? You pushed it open by the doorknob? Or how?

A.: I put my hand up against the door and shoved it open, and went in.
Q.: Did you wipe off the outside of the door then or at any time that day, say, when you were leaving?
A.: Wipe off the outside of the door?
Q.: Wipe your fingerprints off the outside of the door, then or at any time that day?
A.: No.
Q.: You're sure about that?
A.: Yes.
Q.: All right, you're inside the apartment. Describe what happened next.
A.: I didn't see Penny—Penelope—in the living room, so I went to the bedroom. No, first I called out to her again and when there was no answer, then I went to the bedroom.
Q.: Go on.
A.: I saw her lying on the bed. At first I thought she was asleep. I went over to waken her. Then I saw—
Q.: Saw what?
A.: That she was dead.
Q.: How did you know she was dead?
A.: I—you—could tell she wasn't breathing.
Q.: Did you touch her? Touch her body?
A.: Touch her body—?
Q.: Her throat? To see if she had a pulse?
A.: Her throat, no.
Q.: You're sure about that?
A.: Yes.
Q.: And did you see then what had killed her?

A.: The sash, you mean? That was knotted around her throat?

Q.: If that's what you saw. Describe what you saw.

A.: I saw this sash tied tight around her throat. I assumed that's what killed her.

Q.: Where was the sash tied around her throat?

A.: Where? I—it was all around her throat—

Q.: Where was the knot tied?

A.: The knot? I—let me think—I don't think I saw it. I guess I assumed it was tied behind her throat, in back.

Q.: She was lying face up on the bed, fully clothed?

A.: Yes, she was lying on her back. She had her clothes on.

Q.: Describe her clothing.

A.: She had on a—a sweater and skirt—

Q.: Shoes and stockings?

A.: Stockings only, I think. I don't think she had on her shoes.

Q.: Stockings only, you say, no shoes. You're sure about that? Could she have had one shoe on and one shoe off?

A.: She could have. I don't know.

Q.: Go on.

A.: When I saw she was dead, I turned and left the apartment.

Q.: No, let's go back to where you're standing beside the bed. You see that she's dead, you see the sash knotted around her throat—did you recognize the sash?

A.: Recognize it?
Q.: Yes. Did you recognize the sash?
A.: Why would I?
Q.: Because it belonged to a robe you bought for her, a robe that was hanging in her closet. We traced the purchase of the robe to you. You bought it ten days before she moved out on you.
A.: So I bought her the robe, what's the point of the question?
Q.: The question is: Did you recognize the sash as coming from that robe?
A.: I—just don't know. I still don't see the point—
Q.: Let's move on to another question. You're standing beside the bed, you see she's dead, that someone has strangled her—what's the first thought that popped into your head?
A.: The first thought?
Q.: Yes. Did you think of picking up the phone and calling the police?
A.: No, no, I didn't. My thought was that someone had killed her and was trying to frame me. I told you earlier—
Q.: And that was your first thought?
A.: No, that was the thought I had when I thought of calling the police. My first thought was how terrible it was that she was dead.
Q.: And your second thought was that someone was trying to frame you?

A.: Yes, and that's when I decided to get out as fast as possible. And I did.
Q.: Why would anyone want to frame you for her murder?
A.: Because of my belief that I know who killed my father and I intend to pursue the matter and whoever killed Penny wants to frame me for the murder to get me out of the way.
Q.: When we searched your apartment, we found a gun there, a thirty-eight revolver—
A.: I showed you that it's licensed to me in Illinois.
Q.: Why did you bring it to New York?
A.: It was just among my things when Penny and I took an apartment and moved here. Besides, she wasn't shot—
Q.: Let's get back to a couple of earlier questions. First, about the sash again. I can think of a good reason why you might not want to say that you recognized it. That it came from that particular robe that you bought for her.
A.: Why is that?
Q.: Because that particular robe was hanging in the back of her closet. And the sash to it, the sash that strangled her, fits inside the robe except for two small slits in the front where it ties.
A.: I don't see—
Q.: The point is that only someone who knew the robe and the way the sash fits inside it would know the sash was there—as you

would have known. Is that why you say now that you didn't recognize it?

A.: I said I didn't recognize it because I didn't recognize it.

Q.: Let's get back to another earlier question. I asked you if you tried to wipe your fingerprints off the door after you opened it or before you left. You said no. Is that correct?

A.: That's correct.

Q.: Yet, when our lab people went over the whole apartment and the door, they found that someone had tried to wipe everything clean. Doesn't that strike you as odd, that someone would do that if they were trying to frame you?

A.: Not necessarily, no. They could have done it to make it look like I had done it. Make me look guiltier.

Q.: Could have come back to the apartment and wiped it clean after you had been there?

A.: Yes. They could have.

Q.: Sure they could have. But it seems to me it would have been better to have left your prints intact, if they were trying to frame you.

A.: They could have been trying to be doubly sure they'd removed all of their own fingerprints from the place, and removed mine along with them.

Q.: Earlier, too, I asked you if you touched the body, the throat. And you said no. Perhaps you're not aware that these days the lab people can raise fingerprints from human skin. We have two of yours, the thumb and forefinger of your right hand which were taken from the skin of Penelope Lattimore's throat. You must have been feeling for a pulse—to make certain she was dead. At one time or the other.

A.: All I can say is that if I did, I don't remember doing it. I admit I was in somewhat of a state of shock.

Q.: Incidentally, whoever tried to wipe the place clean did a lousy job of it. Even though most of the outside of the door was wiped clean, two more of your prints were found there, from the third and fourth fingers of your right hand.

A.: Since I told you I opened the door, I'm not surprised that they'd be there.

Q.: I have no more questions for now. Do you have anything you want to add?

A.: Not beyond what I've told you. Somebody is trying to frame me.

Q.: You will be available for further questioning?

A.. Yes.

2. CAUSE OF DEATH

WOUND CHART

DECEASED Benjamin C. Robins
MEANS EMPLOYED Gunshot
ADDRESS 42 Sutton Place, Manhattan Apt. #21-D
PLACE/TIME/DATE OF OCCURRENCE About 7 P.M. 12/13
HOM. SGT. #017 DISTRICT 5#11 61 #88703 PCT. 15
DETECTIVE ASSIGNED Whitner SHIELD #7601
C.O.D. Apparent suicide
AUTOPSY BY Dr. E. Allan DATE 12/18 ME #10974 . . .

3. Q. AND A.

Q.: Please state your full name for the record.
A.: Julian Edmund Shields.
Q.: You have read and signed—of your own free will—the Miranda waiver?
A.: I have.
Q.: I have two sets of questions to ask you. The first concerns Penelope Lattimore of Eleven-nineteen East Sixth Street, Manhattan. You knew her?
A.: I did. She became known to me and my wife and several of my associates earlier this year, in France.
Q.: And you continued your friendship with her

after she and you and your wife and associates returned to New York?
A.: I did. She had formed a relationship with Benjamin Robins who also was known to my wife, my associates, and me.
Q.: I come now to the day of December eleventh. Did you receive a phone call from her that day?
A.: I did. She phoned me at my office at Robins Cosmetics.
Q.: And what did she have to say?
A.: She said it was urgent that she see me that day at her apartment.
Q.: And did you go to her apartment?
A.: I did. I received the call in midmorning and, as I told her on the phone, I could not get there until about one o'clock, which I did.
Q.: You arrived at her apartment at one o'clock?
A.: Approximately, yes.
Q.: And what happened then?
A.: She was waiting for me.
Q.: And what did she have to say to you?
A.: She was—what I would call extremely agitated. She told me that Benjamin Robins had been calling her constantly and that she had kept hanging up on him. I had known before that of course that they had broken up.
Q.: Did she tell you the reason why they had broken up?
A.: She had told me that reason sometime be-

fore, as she had told others: that she had become frightened of his behavior.

Q.: Frightened how?

A.: Of his wild talk. His ravings about how he was going to—and I quote her—get even with me and with Charles Robins because he believed we or one of us was responsible for his father's death. Which was of course preposterous, I might add. At least as far as I am concerned in that matter.

Q.: So she had told you this before; what did she have to say that particular day, December eleventh?

A.: She repeated many of the same things she'd already told me about Benjamin Robins. The reason she was so upset on that particular day was because, she said, Benjamin had been calling her repeatedly the past day and all night long and, before she could hang up on him, he screamed the vile things he was going to do to Charles and me.

Q.: Did you believe her story, that this was true about Benjamin Robins?

A.: I—suspect he may have said those things. I never had any reason to doubt her, to imagine she'd made them up. As to whether Benjamin Robins would actually try to do anything, well, I guessed he was just sounding off. That was my opinion.

Q.: But not hers?

A.: No, definitely not hers. Correctly or not, she

was genuinely terrified of him. And I think she was quite sincere in believing he meant to harm me, and Charles Robins.

Q.: And that's all you discussed?

A.: No, there was one other matter. She, Penny, knew that my wife and I and some others, including Charles and his wife, planned to leave in a few days to spend the Christmas holidays in England. Charles's family left him a place there where we all plan to stay. Penny asked if she might go back home along with us—she was from England, you know. I told her yes, she could go with us. She seemed relieved.

Q.: That was the extent of your conversation?

A.: Yes.

Q.: How was she dressed when you were with her?

A.: Dressed? In a—ah—sweater and skirt.

Q.: Shoes and stockings?

A.: Shoes and stockings, too, yes.

Q.: And then you left her?

A.: Yes.

Q.: And that was what time, approximately?

A.: One-thirty, one-forty-five, I would say.

Q.: And you never returned to her apartment that day?

A.: No, I did not.

Q.: Can you think of anything else you'd like to tell us about Penelope Lattimore?

A.: I can't think of anything else.

Q.: Now I would like to discuss the death of Benjamin Robins.
A.: Yes?
Q.: When did you first learn of his death?
A.: When your people, the police, contacted me at my apartment that evening and told me. The evening of December thirteenth.
Q.: Exactly what were you told?
A.: That he had been found alone in his apartment, a gun in his hand, a bullet through his head, and that there was a note left, a suicide note.
Q.: A typewritten note, unsigned.
A.: Yes, I was told that.
Q.: Do you think he committed suicide?
A.: It would seem that way, especially if, as I understand, the typewritten note confesses that he killed Penny Lattimore.
Q.: Even though the note was unsigned?
A.: I cannot speculate on that.
Q.: As you know, his body was found at approximately seven P.M. on that date by patrolmen responding to a call reporting the sound of a gunshot in the building. Benjamin Robins was here at this precinct being interrogated that same day until about three in the afternoon. Mr. Shields, where were you between the hours of three and seven P.M. on December thirteenth?
A.: As I told your officers when they first asked me that question, I was in my office at

Robins Cosmetics. Until about five o'clock, and then I walked home, as is my custom, to my apartment on Park Avenue. My wife and I live there when we have to be in the city, away from our home in Maryland. I arrived at the apartment between six and six-fifteen, as well as I can figure.

Q.: I have no further questions, Mr. Shields.

A.: As you know, we're leaving for England in a few days—

Q.: Yes, we know. If we have any additional questions, we'll call you before then. And we have the address where you'll be staying in England, in the event that additional questions arise.

4. Q. AND A.

Q.: Please state your full name for the record.

A.: Charles Atherton Robins.

Q.: You have read the Miranda waiver and, of your own free will, signed it?

A.: I have.

Q.: I have two sets of questions to ask you. The first concerns Penelope Lattimore of Eleven-nineteen East Sixth Street, Manhattan. You knew her?

A.: Yes. First in England, where we saw one another frequently. And later in France, and then here in America.

Q.: You remained friends?

A.: Quite.
Q.: When was the last time you saw her?
A.: In the afternoon of December eleventh, when I went to her apartment.
Q.: How did you happen to go to her apartment that particular day?
A.: She kept phoning me frantically off and on all morning.
Q.: And she told you she wanted to see you?
A.: She told my wife, Genevieve, actually. She, Penny, couldn't reach me. I was at the Robins Cosmetics laboratories in New Jersey all morning or en route back to New York. I just recently joined the company, and they've kept me busy. So Penny kept calling Genevieve.
Q.: What did she say to her, to your wife?
A.: Penny appeared to my wife to be distraught; she kept telling her that I was in danger, that Benjamin Robins was going to do something terrible to me. She had to see me.
Q.: She told your wife all this over the phone?
A.: Yes. By the time I got back to the city in the afternoon and called my wife, *she* was practically beside herself as well. Penny had scared her half to death with her phone calls.
Q.: What did you do?
A.: Genevieve, my wife, insisted that I see Penny at once. I tried to phone the apartment but the line was busy. So I drove down there.

Q.: What time was this?
A.: About four or four-fifteen, approximately.
Q.: And you hadn't been there earlier that day?
A.: No. I told you I was in New Jersey and then driving back to the city.
Q.: Alone?
A.: Alone.
Q.: So you got to her apartment about four or so. Describe what happened.
A.: I went to her apartment. The door was closed. I knocked, and when there was no answer, I tried the doorknob and found the door was unlocked. I went in.
Q.: Describe what you saw.
A.: I found Penny lying on the bed in her bedroom. There was a colored scarf twisted around her throat. I could see she was dead.
Q.: How was she dressed?
A.: Sweater, skirt, stockings, one shoe on, one shoe off. It's all still vivid to me.
Q.: Had you ever seen the sash, the scarf, that was around her neck?
A.: No, never.
Q.: What did you do then?
A.: I picked up the phone and called the police. Then I waited until they arrived.
Q.: Did you touch anything in the apartment that day?
A.: Touch anything? No.
Q.: Had you ever visited her in her apartment before?
A.: Alone? No. My wife and I stopped by there

together to see her the day she moved in—
what, three weeks or so ago.
Q.: The police laboratory discovered your fingerprints on a whiskey glass on a shelf in the kitchen. Any idea how they got there?
A.: Glass? Oh, wait! Before the police came, I went in the kitchen and took down a glass and had a drink of water. I remember now. I was pretty shaken.
Q.: And you had never visited her alone in her apartment before that day?
A.: No, as I told you.
Q.: Did you take these threats of Benjamin Robins against you seriously?
A.: No. Although my wife did want me to inform the police. She said Benjamin had to be stopped or he'd kill me. I didn't know how much of what Penny was saying was just her imagination. She could be quite hysterical at times.
Q.: Do you think she wanted to cause trouble in your marriage? After all, you and she once were close, and now she and Benjamin Robins had split up.
A.: No. There was nothing like that.
Q.: Do you have anything you'd like to tell us about the death of Penelope Lattimore?
A.: Nothing I can think of.
Q.: Now I'd like to ask you about the death of Benjamin Robins; you know all the facts, I believe.
A.: His suicide? I presume I know all the facts.

Q.: His apparent suicide. On the day his death occurred, December thirteenth, where were you between the hours of three and seven P.M.?

A.: Would you believe, most of that time I was driving back to New York from New Jersey. As you know, I have told the police this before.

Q.: Alone?

A.: Alone.

Q.: And what time did you reach your apartment? When the police tried to call you there, there was no answer.

A.: Actually, I didn't go to my apartment directly when I got back to the city. I met my wife in the Edwardian Room at the Plaza Hotel. Our date was for seven-thirty. Actually, I arrived early. About seven. I had several drinks at the bar there while waiting for my wife. The bartender there knows me. He can verify the time. We—I—didn't know about Benjamin's death until eleven or so when we got back to the apartment.

Q.: I have no further questions at this time, Mr. Robins.

A.: As you know, we're leaving for England—

Q.: Yes, in a few days, we know. If we have any additional questions, we'll be in touch with you, here or there.

CHAPTER 8

A BLUNT INSTRUMENT

THE IDEA FOR CELEBRATING THE Christmas holidays in England, with Julian and Janice Shields present, along with David and Pamela McGuffin, the remaining members of the Taylor Robins family: Rebecca, Jonathan, Laura, Daphne, and Dorothy—as well as Paul Bryce—originated with Captain Gregory Waltham. However, no one knew this except Charles and Genevieve Robins.

All had been invited to stay at the Atherton ancestral home, Riverham Manor, in the countryside of England, where Charles had grown up, a house he had inherited when his grandfather, Lord Robert Atherton, had died. Captain Waltham would be there, too.

Captain Waltham had conceived the idea of bringing them all together after the death of Penny Lattimore and the apparent suicide of Benjamin Robins. Waltham had become quite obsessed by the cases but had not been able to spend much time investigating this series of murders because of his duties with the Maryland State Police. Finally, so driven was he to unravel the enigma that he had taken early retirement from the Maryland police to devote his full energies to solving the crimes. He had had the inspiration of gathering together all those who might be suspects. When he had discussed the plan with Charles and Genevieve, they had agreed to participate, and to provide the setting, Riverham Manor.

The great old house, which had once been a showcase of the Atherton family, had fallen into disrepair in recent years after the death of Lord Robert and the subsequent decline in the fortunes of Charles and his late mother. But since the marriage of Charles and Genevieve, she had supplied the necessary funds to restore Riverham Manor to at least a semblance of its former splendor. In addition, she and Charles had arranged for a full staff to work there during the Christmas holidays, if not longer: two cooks, a butler, two serving maids, a chauffeur, and a handyman.

So all was in readiness by the time the guests arrived from America, on the day before Christmas Eve, as it happened. Almost as if on cue, heavy snow began to fall that evening only hours after Julian and Janice, the last of the guests, arrived. With roaring fires in all the great stone fireplaces in the house, Riverham became a comforting haven indeed.

"Our house may not be as grand as Greenlawn," Charles remarked to Julian, "but please think of it as your English home away from home."

"It's a lovely place," Julian answered after he had made a tour of the house with Charles. "Once inside here, one feels one has taken a step back into an earlier century. Your grandfather must have been an adventurous gentleman, as well."

This last remark by Julian was prompted by the fact that the two of them were standing in the library of Riverham Manor where mounted upon the walls was an awesome display of ancient and modern hunting weapons. The collection included a crossbow, an African blowgun, a broadsword, a spike-studded wooden club, an Indian pigsticker, several rifles, a pair of crossed spears, and a machete.

"Grandfather collected them on his trips around the world," Charles explained, making light of them. "Actually, I don't think he ever went hunting in his life. This collection was something of a put-on, I suspect. They made good conversation pieces in his day."

That evening all the guests lingered long at the dining-room table which was heaped high with dishes of poached salmon, ham, venison, Yorkshire pudding, a variety of steaming vegetables, and baskets of fresh-baked bread.

The presence of Captain Gregory Waltham at Riverham Manor had, at first, created an atmosphere of unease among a few of those present because of his official interest in some of the past murders that had touched them. Charles had explained that he had invited Waltham to celebrate the captain's retirement from police work; that the two of them had become friends while Charles was in America and had frequently discussed the murders. During the course of the dinner, Waltham used his considerable charm to put the others at ease in his company. By the time desserts had been served and the last of the wine drunk, they were all relaxed with one another.

After dinner, drinks were served in the library where the handyman had stacked a supply of wood next to the huge fireplace already ablaze with crackling logs. Outside the windows, where the drapes were open, falling snow obscured the countryside beyond. In front of one row of windows stood a giant spruce tree, reaching to the ceiling of the room and in dark silhouette, awaiting the following day and its Christmas trimmings.

As soon as the group was settled around the fire, drinks in hand, Charles proposed that they play a game of word association, a suggestion secretly made to Charles and Genevieve by Captain Waltham. The captain hoped that in this disarming manner someone present might inadvertently let slip a word that could be a clue to the murders.

To start the game, the first person in the circle—in this instance, Charles—spoke a word, which the person next to him immediately had to answer with another word, this second word being the one that sprang to mind, by association, with the first word. The person who was to answer had to do so at once or be passed over. Once the associated word was given, the person answering had then to announce yet another word associated with the answer given.

With Charles sitting in the center, the circle was composed of Genevieve on his left, then Rebecca, Jonathan, Laura, Paul Bryce, Daphne, David MacGuffin,

Pamela, Julian, Janice, Waltham, and Dorothy, completing the circle, on Charles's right.

"Color," Charles said.

"White," Genevieve answered, and said, "Snow."

"Fall," Rebecca answered, and said, "Leaves."

"Tree," Jonathan answered, and said, "Logs."

"Fire," Laura answered, and said, "Uh—ah—sirens."

"Street," Bryce answered, and said, "Sidewalk."

"People," Daphne answered, shook her head, blushed, and stammered, "I—uh—pass."

"People," MacGuffin quickly repeated, answered, "Us," and said, "Friends."

Pamela blinked her eyes and said, "Pass."

"Friends," Julian repeated quickly, answered, "Remembered," and said, "Past." He hurriedly added, "That's p-a-s-t. Past."

"Years," Janice answered, and said, "Life."

"Death," Waltham answered without hesitation, and said, "Murder."

"Oh, look here now—" Jonathan started to protest. Charles cut him off, saying, "It's only a game, Jonathan. What's the matter?"

Jonathan stood up. "It's a silly game, if that's what it is. It looks like a trick to me." He pointed to Captain Waltham. "He just wants to get us onto the subject of murder, so he can see what we say."

"Playing the game was my suggestion," Charles reminded Jonathan mildly.

"I just spoke the first thing that came to mind," Waltham said, fiddling with his hearing aid.

"I still say it's a silly game," Jonathan persisted. "I've had enough of it." He stalked over to the sideboard and splashed brandy into his glass.

Charles shrugged. "Well, if any of the rest of you feel that way, perhaps we should forget the game."

"It isn't that I have any objection to continuing the game for that reason," Rebecca murmured, perhaps in a gesture to mollify her son, Jonathan, "but it has been a long day. I think I'm quite ready to retire."

A short while later, with the fire in the library dying into ashes, the group made its way upstairs and to bed.

The next day the snow was still falling and it continued into the evening. Before dinner was served, Charles and Genevieve, helped by most of the others in the group, completed decorating the Christmas tree. After dinner, they all went to their rooms to collect the presents they'd brought, to place them under the tree.

Captain Waltham, after going to his room, remained there for a while, making notes on the three by five cards for the file he had brought along with him. When he had completed the task, he went back downstairs, his arms loaded with packages.

When he reached the library, some of the others were already there, although at first he could not make out who they were since the room was darkly shadowed, the only light coming from the tiny sparkling and blinking colored lights on the Christmas tree and from the fireplace where the fire had burned low. Then his eyes adjusted to the room's dim light, aided additionally by the fresh logs just placed in the fireplace whose roaring flames funneled up the chimney. He saw that Charles and Genevieve were by the tree, Pamela was standing in front of one of the windows—where the drapes were still open—looking out at the falling snow, and David MacGuffin and Paul Bryce were together feeding the fresh logs into the fireplace.

Waltham had just finished placing his presents under the tree when Rebecca Robins and her three daughters came through the door, followed by Janice Shields, all of them also laden down with presents that they arranged beneath the tree.

When Janice moved away from the tree, she looked around the dimly lit room and asked, in a puzzled voice, "Where's Julian? He came down some time ago."

"He was here earlier," Charles said. "I saw him here about forty minutes ago. I was here, too, and then I went back upstairs to pick up a package I had forgotten. Come to think of it, I don't remember seeing him here when I returned with Genevieve."

"He didn't come back upstairs," Janice said. "Wherever can he be?"

"And Jonathan, too," Rebecca Robins said, looking around the room. "Where is he? He came down quite a while ago. Close to an hour ago he knocked on my door in passing and said he'd be in the library."

When Captain Waltham heard the words of the two women, he experienced an intuitive sense of foreboding.

Paul Bryce said, "I passed Jonathan on the stairs. He was headed back up to his room as I was coming down. That was about fifteen minutes ago. Julian wasn't here when I arrived. The room was empty."

"Both Julian and Jonathan were here when I left," Charles said in further explanation.

Hearing all these reports, Waltham suggested that the house be searched for the two men. Charles, Janice, and Rebecca started out of the room just as Jonathan appeared.

"Where have you been?" Rebecca asked. "I thought you came down an hour ago."

Jonathan appeared surprised. "I went back to my room to change my clothes. Earlier, when I was here, I spilled wine on my suit jacket."

"Have you seen Julian?" Waltham's question came out more brusquely than he had intended.

"Julian?" Jonathan repeated. "Yes, he was here in the library when I left."

"Well, he's not here now," Janice said and then she and Charles went on out of the room to search the house. Rebecca, now that Jonathan was accounted for, remained there.

Waltham could not shake his feeling that something was seriously amiss. He started to wander over toward the windows and, partway there, suddenly stopped, peering down at the carpeting on the floor where there was a large dark stain.

He couldn't make out what the stain was, even when he knelt closer to see. "Can't we have some more light in here?" he asked irritably.

"Yes, of course," Genevieve answered quickly, going to the light switch.

"Much better," Waltham muttered, as the room was flooded with light. He could see now that the stain on the rug was a large round circle.

"If you're wondering what that is," Jonathan said, coming over, "that's where I spilled my glass of wine."

"Hmm," Waltham said.

A shrill scream pierced the air in the next second. Pamela was the one who had screamed. She was still standing close to the window and pointing to a corner of the room where the open drapes were gathered in folds. They all saw what she had seen first. A man's foot protruded from the drape folds.

Waltham moved quickly, crossing to the corner and thrusting the drapes aside to reveal Julian Shields lying on his back on the floor, eyes closed. There was a pool of blood beneath his head.

Waltham spent a brief time bent over the body, then announced softly: "He's dead. It appears he suffered a wound to the back of his head. The police must be called at once."

The local police sergeant, whose name was Peter Gully, and two other policemen reached the house within half an hour.

As soon as Sergeant Gully was apprised of the circumstances at Riverham Manor, he used the phone to call New Scotland Yard in London. "This requires the presence of an inspector," Gully explained to Waltham who had meanwhile identified himself as a former police officer.

"Now we have to clear this room and wait," Gully informed all of them. "They'll be along in time."

The sergeant posted a man at the closed door of the library, he and the other man with him going to the dining room where they questioned everyone who had been in the house. Janice, who was being cared for by Genevieve, remained in her bedroom.

Some time passed before a squad of policemen arrived from New Scotland Yard, among them members of the forensic unit and several uniformed men, led by Inspector Malcolm Toliver.

It didn't take them long to arrive at certain tentative conclusions about the murder. The forensic unit soon determined that Julian had died of a blow to the back of his skull, delivered by, in their words, "a blunt instrument." In his right hand they found a coat button.

They had already noted, from descriptions given of the normal appearance of the room, that the spike-studded wooden club—usually to be found hanging on the wall—was missing. Nor did it take them long to find the missing club just outside one of the library windows where it had been thrown into the snow.

"All we have to do now," Inspector Toliver confided briskly to Captain Waltham, "is to find out who wielded the death weapon. I am reminded," he added, "of those apt lines of Edmund Spenser: 'A foggy mist had covered all the land; and underneath their feet, all scattered lay dead skulls and bones of men whose life had gone astray.' Appropriate, don't you think?"

"Appropriate, yes." Waltham nodded, although, he thought, he might not have phrased it so; but then he'd never been a British policeman.

Inspector Toliver was nevertheless all business when he got down to cross-examining his subjects. Jonathan Robins became the prime suspect almost at once based upon various statements of those who had been in and out of the library that day.

Charles Robins, who had been the first one to place himself in the library while Julian was there, stated:

"Both Julian and Jonathan were in the library together while I was there and when I left."

Jonathan Robins stated: "Julian was still there when I left to change my jacket after I spilled wine on it."

Paul Bryce stated: "Julian was not in sight in the library when I got there. I never thought of searching the room for him. Actually, it was quite dark in the room and I decided to build up the fire." Bryce paused before he added: "Before I reached the library, I passed Jonathan going upstairs. I noticed wine stains on his jacket and that one of his jacket buttons was missing."

David MacGuffin stated: "When I reached the library, there was no sign of Julian. I helped Paul Bryce put logs on the fire, which is what we were doing when Captain Waltham got there and, soon afterward, the others."

After taking these statements, Inspector Toliver called Jonathan back for requestioning, confronting him with the words of Charles Robins, Paul Bryce, and David MacGuffin, and the coat button found in Julian's hand.

During this interrogation, Jonathan changed his story, admitting: "After Charles left the library, when Julian and I were alone, we had words. I admit I got carried away and accused him of having something to do with my father's death. Julian became furious with me. He knocked the full wineglass from my hands, some of the wine spilling on my jacket, the rest on the rug. He grabbed the front of my jacket at the same time. That's when the button ripped off, although I thought the button fell on the floor at the time. I was so upset I left the room without looking for it. But when I left, Julian was alive."

Once Jonathan had concluded his second statement, Inspector Toliver met alone with Captain Waltham, asking for details about the murder of Jonathan's father, Taylor Robins. Waltham gave the inspector all the facts.

"He's our man, all right, then," Inspector Toliver said. "Jonathan, the murderer of Julian Shields. I'm taking him in for further questioning, along with that club we found in the snow. Unless I miss my guess, we'll find Julian Shields's blood on it once it's gone through the lab."

Soon after, the police left, with Jonathan—protesting—in custody. And they took with them the spike-studded wooden club. Inspector Toliver left two of his men behind to guard the library which he wanted kept sealed until the investigation ended.

While the rest of those in the house retired for the night, Captain Waltham stayed awake in his room, poring over all the facts he'd managed to amass about all the murders that had taken place so far, facts he had noted on his 3 by 5 file cards and in certain tape recordings he had made without the knowledge of those speaking. And here it can be revealed for the first time that the hearing aid worn by Captain Gregory Waltham was, in fact, not a hearing aid at all! It was a microphone which led to a tiny recorder concealed in Waltham's pocket. This device allowed him to record almost everything that went on around him.

In addition, Waltham had new facts that had come into his hands since Inspector Toliver had departed: David MacGuffin had brought to Waltham copies he'd had made of the contents of Evelyn Robins's diary and of the tape recording of the conversation, so long ago, between Paul Bryce and Tyler Robins. The originals of the diary and the tape rested in a safe-deposit box in New York City, MacGuffin explained to Waltham, but he had brought copies with him because he had begun to write a novel based upon the murders.

During all of that long Christmas Eve night, Captain Waltham pondered the murder of Julian Shields and how all the facts he had before him might provide a solution to Julian's murder, if not to all the other murders. Twice during the night, he had put in phone calls to Scotland Yard, to Inspector Toliver, who also was working through the night. Once Waltham called to ask if the laboratory had found any blood on the spike-studded club. The inspector reported that tests so far had been negative. The second time Waltham phoned the inspector to ask a series of very technical forensic questions. He had to wait on the phone until Toliver could find the answers. Then Waltham returned to his task of solving Julian's murder.

At dawn, Waltham, weary but exhilarated, phoned Toliver for yet a third time. On this call, Waltham urgently requested Toliver to return to Riverham Manor as soon as possible and to bring Jonathan Robins with him. Toliver was reluctant but Waltham impressed upon him that the matter was of the utmost importance.

Christmas morning was just dawning when Inspector Toliver and one of his men drove Jonathan back to the house.

Captain Waltham had already roused everyone else in the house and, once the inspector was present, asked all of them to assemble in the library once again.

When they had all taken seats in the room, Captain

Waltham paced back and forth, saying, "I am now going to explain to you how Julian Shields was murdered, who murdered him, and the motive for his murder."

He walked over and stood in front of Charles Robins. "You," Waltham said, "claim that when you left the library, Julian and Jonathan were there."

Charles nodded.

Waltham walked over and stood in front of Jonathan. "You," Waltham said, "claim that you and Julian had a heated argument during which wine spilled on the carpet and a button was ripped from your coat. But that Julian was alive when you left the room."

Jonathan nodded.

Waltham walked over and stood in front of Paul Bryce. "You," Waltham said, "claim that Julian was not in sight here in the room when you got here."

Paul Bryce nodded.

Waltham walked over and stood in front of David MacGuffin. "And you," Waltham said, "claim that Julian was not in sight in the room when you got here, that you helped Paul Bryce build up the fire which is what you were doing when I arrived."

MacGuffin nodded.

Waltham resumed pacing back and forth across the room, addressing the group as a whole, much as if they were a jury.

"You will notice," he said, "that according to their individual statements, Julian was said to be in the room while Charles was here and while Jonathan was here. But not to be here, or in sight, when Paul Bryce arrived or when David MacGuffin arrived."

Waltham paused, put a hand up to his hearing aid, then continued: "One assumption, then, is that Julian was killed by the last man to admit seeing him alive, who is Jonathan, or that Julian was killed between the time Jonathan departed and Paul Bryce arrived, followed by David MacGuffin."

Waltham paused, thought for a moment, and said, "Before we go on with this line of reasoning, let's talk for a moment about the false clues that are a part of any murder case, clues that appear to lead inexorably to a correct solution of the case, but don't. False clues. In fictional murder mysteries they are called"—he smiled slightly—"'red herrings.'"

Waltham walked back and stood in front of Jonathan. "You have heard," he said, "that Paul Bryce passed you on the stairs after you admit you had had a heated argument with Julian. Paul noticed that the front of your jacket was covered with wine and that a button was missing."

Jonathan nodded.

Waltham walked over and stood in front of Paul Bryce. "You came downstairs after passing Jonathan," Waltham said, "and entered the library."

Paul Bryce nodded.

Waltham once more addressed the group in the room as a whole.

"Now," he said, "we come to how red herrings can be employed to divert suspicion away from the real guilty party in a murder case. Think about it: Paul Bryce enters the library; he's looking for, and sees, the spilled wine on the carpet, and Jonathan's missing coat button there, too, on the carpet. Paul Bryce makes a small detour and then continues across the room. He comes up behind Julian who is standing at the window, looking out, probably troubled by the earlier scene with Jonathan, and then Paul Bryce crushes the back of Julian's skull with the murder weapon and places the body behind the drapes."

There was a soft collective sigh from those listening in the room.

"And then," Inspector Toliver suggested softly, "Bryce goes to the window, opens it, and pitches the spike-studded club outside into the snow."

Captain Waltham shook his head. "No. Paul Bryce makes a small detour before he goes to the spike-studded club hanging on the wall, takes it down, and tosses it out the window into the snow."

"And then?" the question came from Jonathan.

"And then, and only then," Waltham said, "does Paul Bryce hurry back to where he's placed the murder weapon—and I might add, barely has time to get rid of it before David MacGuffin walks in on him. In fact, MacGuffin, unknowingly, actually observes Bryce destroying the real murder weapon. I refer of course to a log Paul Bryce had just fed to the fire, one of several he, and MacGuffin still unknowingly, placed on the fire."

"You can't prove any of this," Paul Bryce blurted out.

"Yes, I can," Waltham said. "But first, I want to discuss the motive for Julian's murder, as I said I would. The seeds for it were planted long ago, as is often what happens. Before Evelyn Robins died she kept a diary and had in her possession a tape recording of a conversation between her husband and you, Paul Bryce. For a long time after her death, both were missing. Now they have reappeared."

Waltham paused to look at Bryce. "I have copies of both of them. They reveal that Paul Bryce stole plans for new products from Robins Cosmetics. Tyler Robins had proof of this fact. B. J. Grieg, the private detective, produced this proof. Grieg, incidentally, may have been blackmailing Bryce before Grieg was murdered. At one time Robins Cosmetics was going to bring charges against Bryce. After Julian Shields became head of Robins Cosmetics, the case was dropped—presumably because the diary and the tape could not be found. Yet, according to Evelyn's diary, Julian knew about the tape—and what's even more important, Julian knew about the documents that proved Bryce's guilt, documents that Tyler Robins had in his possession. When Tyler Robins died and Julian took over as head of Robins Cosmetics, those documents came into Julian's possession."

Waltham was quiet for a moment before he said, "Julian could have used those documents to take Paul Bryce to court. But he didn't. Julian wanted money for his personal use, to rebuild Greenlawn, for example; he used the documents, as Grieg perhaps did, *to blackmail Paul Bryce. And that's why Paul Bryce killed Julian Shields right here in this room!*"

Waltham returned to stand in front of Bryce again, pointing to the gray ashes in the fireplace from the night before. "You're wrong if you think it can't be proved that you murdered Julian. You were seen placing the log in the fire, you had the motive, everyone else in this room before you came in, saw Julian alive. What's more to the point, I have been assured that forensic science can recover the presence of blood from those ashes and match it with Julian's blood type."

Paul Bryce seemed to wilt at that moment and a short while later was led away by Inspector Toliver, after the inspector had congratulated Waltham warmly.

Waltham's last statement to Paul Bryce was untrue. Waltham was bluffing. He had been told that it was impossible to determine scientifically the presence of blood and tissue once they had been exposed to fire. Paul Bryce had stumbled upon the perfect way to destroy a murder weapon but he did not know this. Besides, Waltham *had* established Bryce's motive for committing the murder, the method he had used, and above all else, the opportunity he—and he alone—had to commit the murder. These facts would almost surely convict Bryce in a court of law.

One month later, after everyone else had returned to America, Paul Bryce in England confessed to the murder of Julian Shields.

During the year that followed, Janice Shields decided to sell the Greenlawn estate in Maryland and return to England to live. Charles Robins, who had meanwhile been elected chairman of Robins Cosmetics, and Genevieve, bought the estate. Once more there was a Robins at the head of Robins Cosmetics and a Robins family living at Greenlawn.

Carrie Wales and her daughter, Molly, moved away from Greenlawn and haven't been heard from since, although they draw money from a trust arranged by Charles, who wanted to carry out Evelyn's wishes.

Captain Gregory Waltham went into business for himself as a private investigator and is on a retainer from Robins Cosmetics for his services whenever needed. In his spare time, Waltham continues to be obsessed by the unsolved murders and devotes hours each day to attempting to solve them.

David MacGuffin and Pamela live in Princeton, New Jersey, where MacGuffin, in addition to serving on the board of directors of Robins Cosmetics, is in charge of the research laboratories. MacGuffin spends his spare time writing a mystery novel based upon the eight murders contained in this account. He hopes they will be solved before he reaches the end of the book. He is, however, satisfied with the first few lines he wrote at the opening of the novel:

Invitation to Murder
The invitation, on a plain white card, read:

ABOUT THE AUTHORS

Bill Adler is the country's foremost book packager and publishing innovator.

In the literary field, he has represented such authors as President Ronald Reagan, Nancy Reagan, Mike Wallace, Dan Rather, Phil Donahue, Howard Cosell, Helen Hayes, Steve Allen, Hugh Downs, Margaret Truman, Pat Collins, Dick Clark, Ralph Nader, Charles Osgood, Jessica Savitch, George Gallup, Jr., Senator William S. Cohen, Gene Tierney, Dr. Lee Salk, Gene Autry, Ron Nessen, Larry King, Joan Lunden, Art Linkletter, Pat Boone, Bess Myerson, Phyllis George, Willard Scott, Robert MacNeil, and Senator Gary Hart.

As an author, Bill Adler has had more than fifty-eight books published, including such national best sellers as *The I Love New York Diet* (with Bess Myerson), *Letters from Camp, Kids' Letters to President Kennedy, The Kennedy Wit,* and *Inside Publishing.*

He has also been an editor at *McCall's* magazine, the editorial director of Playboy's book division, and host of the network television program *Kid Talk.*

Bill Adler was the creator of the phenomenal number-one best seller *Who Killed the Robins Family?*

Mr. Adler is married, has two children, and lives in New York.

Thomas Chastain has lived and worked in New York City, Baltimore, and Hollywood as a newspaper reporter and editor, advertising copywriter, and magazine writer and editor before turning full time to writing fiction.

Mr. Chastain is the author of a series of suspense novels including *Pandora's Box, 911, Vital Statistics, High Voltage, The Diamond Exchange,* and *Nightscape.*

He is on the board of directors of the Mystery Writers of America and has served as chairman of that organization's Edgar Allan Poe Awards.

He was the writer of the phenomenal number-one best seller *Who Killed the Robins Family?*

Mr. Chastain lives with his wife in New York City and is currently at work on a new novel.

Who Killed the Robins Family?, which, when first published, was on the national best-seller lists for more than thirty-five weeks, is now available in a Warner Books paperback edition. In addition to the complete text of the original hardcover book, it contains the authors' solution to the mystery. Warner Books is also offering a $2,500 Bonus Award to the person who provides the winning solution to the *The Revenge of the Robins Family* contest. For Bonus Award eligibility requirements, see the Warner paperback edition of *Who Killed the Robins Family?*

Here Are Additional Clues to Help You Solve the Mystery of THE REVENGE OF THE ROBINS FAMILY and Win $10,001.

Chapter 1:

First to arrive...